Littlest Death

An Afterlife Fantasy

Also by Eric Witchey

Professor Witchey's Miracle Mood Cure. A Collection of 25 mood altering short stories from multiple genres. Seven are previously unpublished.

Neighborhood Tales. Pen Name, E. E. Marshall. A collection of inspirational short stories.

Bull's Labyrinth. A historical fantasy suspense romance about cursed love between Nikkis and the Master Mason Daedalus in ancient Crete, the survival of that love, and how that love finally breaks the curse in modern times.

How I Met My Alien Bitch Lover. A true tabloid tale of alien coyotes, techno-ninjas, and love.

Beyond the Serpent's Heart. A Mayan fantasy novel that tells the tale of why the world didn't end at the end of the Mayan calendar in 2012.

Fighting Mother's Echo. Polish, only. Science Fiction tale of one woman's struggle to make peace with the voices in her head in a future of corporate feudalism and religious media share wars.

To Build a Boat, Listen to Trees. A near-fantasy novelette in which paying attention to the world around us creates justice, love, and belief in magic.

The Tao of Flynn. A near-fantasy novelette in which a mysterious salesman teaches his protégé how to create justice by giving people what they want.

Littlest Death

A Labyrinth of Souls Novel

by

Eric Witchey

ShadowSpinners Press

Cover art by Josephe Vandel.
Book design by Matthew Lowes.

ShadowSpinners Press
shadowspinnerspress.com

Typeset in
Minion Pro by Robert Slimbach
and IM FELL Double Pica by Igino Marini.
The Fell Types are digitally reproduced
by Igino Marini, www.iginomarini.com.

Learn more about
the Labyrinth of Souls game at
matthewlowes.com/games.

For my sister, Leonore, who supported the creation of this little tale in so many ways that I can't begin to list them.

Acknowledgements

As always, the number of people I should thank is endless. Every kindness they have offered has made my effort stronger. However, special thanks for this book go to my sister, Leonore. Without her help, this story would not exist. Thanks also go to Elizabeth Engstrom for her 2x4 encouragement and editorial skills. I want to thank editors and fellow writers Christina Lay and Matt Lowes for creating the Labyrinth of Souls project and including this tale. Finally, I want to thank Sandra Siegiensky for showing up for work, feeding me from time to time, and helping me stay on track.

Table of Contents

EDITOR'S PREFACE

Dungeon Solitaire: Labyrinth of Souls is a fantasy game for tarot cards, written by Matthew Lowes and Illustrated by Josephe Vandel. In the game you defeat monsters, disarm traps, open doors, and explore mazes as you delve the depths of a dangerous dungeon. Along the way you collect treasure and magic items, gain skills, and gather companions.

Now ShadowSpinners Press is publishing this and other stand-alone novels inspired by the game. Each *Labyrinth of Souls* novel features a journey into a unique vision of the underworld.

The Labyrinth of Souls is more than an ancient ruin filled with monsters, trapped treasure, and the lost tombs of bygone kings. It is a manifestation of a mythic underworld, existing at a crossroads between people and cultures, between time and space, between the physical world and the deepest reaches of the psyche. It is a dark mirror held up to human experience, in which you may find your dreams ... or your doom. Entrances to this realm can appear in any time period, in any location. There are innumerable reasons why a person may enter, but it is a place antagonistic to those who do, a place where monsters dwell, with obstacles and illusions to waylay adventurers, and whose very walls can be a force of corruption. It is a haunted place, ever at the edge of sanity.

Littlest Death

An Afterlife Fantasy

In the Deeps

Freezing and alone in the dark ocean depths, Littlest Death stood ankle deep in the bodies of dead plankton and single-celled organisms. Miles of ocean above rained down an eerie snow of the dead and dying creatures that formed the very foundation of all life on Earth.

Diligently, she tapped the rim of her soul-gathering bucket to stop time before she dragged it once more through the interminable glow of millions of soul sparks departing their flesh.

Thus, Littlest Death gathered in millions upon millions of tiny sparks.

When sparks filled her bucket to the brim, she lifted it to her chest to protect it while she trudged along a deep rift arroyo toward the nebulous veil separating Overworld from Underworld.

Cold and dark and pressure were nothing to a death of her caliber, she told herself as she tapped the bucket rim to let time return to the deeps.

Her job done, she slipped from Overworld, the world of flesh, into Underworld, the world of spirit. She carried her bucket with pride. No other death was trusted with millions of souls each trip. Not even Oldest Death, who had given her this assignment over a thousand years ago, carried *millions*.

Certainly, his Ancientness could swing his scythe and retrieve thousands of human souls, but only she carried The Bucket of Bringing and carried millions.

Safely in Underworld, she cast about in the dim, silver-blue light shining from the stream flowing from the Lake of All Souls to the veil. The shimmering souls that made up the river dripped through the veil into Overworld one shining soul at a time to once more find flesh to inhabit.

This was the cycle of life as it had been since before she had become self-aware.

Birth. Death. Return to Underworld and The Lake. Mingle in the knowing of all souls then flow forth into Overworld. Birth, again.

Surrounded by welcoming shadows and embraced by the familiar mingled scent of damp rock, earthen steam, and the field flower sweetness of souls nearing new life, she reveled in her sense of a job well done and began the hike upstream toward the Lake of All Souls.

Her soiled, dripping black robes tangled around her bony ankles, and she tripped. Barely keeping the bucket from spilling millions of sparks onto the black basalt floor of Underworld, she once more cursed the fact that she had not grown into the robes she'd been given a thousand years before.

From the shifting shadows made by the glowing stream through the corridors of stone ahead, a familiar sardonic feline chuckle echoed.

Littlest Death's warm mood of accomplishment disappeared, cooled by the ice of resentment.

Holding the bucket handle by one bone-fingered hand, she gathered up her robes with the other. As quickly as she could without spilling sparks from her precious load, she strode upstream toward ever wider waters.

As she rounded the first bend in the stream, she came face-to-face with two Egyptian deaths: Baast, the cat goddess, and Ammit, the alligator who weighs souls in their metaphor of underworld.

Baast blocked the path, her sleek white and gold robe hanging straight and clean from her Ankh-collared neck to her clawed, sandaled feet.

"Excuse me," Littlest Death said. She shifted to one side, but that meant she had to step over the thick, plated tail of Ammit, who lounged naked, long, and leathery among black stones as if he had no worries in the whole of Overworld or Underworld.

Baast said, "Another bucket full of slime mold, fungi, and amoeba souls?"

Littlest Death shifted nearer the cavern wall in an effort to get by. "Millions," she said. "Millions of souls."

Unimpressed, Baast flashed her fanged, feral smile. "Millions? Truly? So many?"

Littlest Death shielded her precious bucket, pressed herself against the stones, and squeezed between the unmoving and unmoved, enigmatic Baast.

Ammit said, "The bucket must be very heavy."

Baast licked her own furred hand and exhaled a tiny hiss, which shrank her ever so slightly and let Littlest Death squeeze by.

"Your ever so fashionable black robes," the fastidious feline said, "are covered in sludge and muck."

Littlest Death, now free to hurry upstream, suddenly stopped.

Millions of humans believing you had a shape gave you a shape, but it didn't mean you worked harder. Littlest had worked hard to fill her bucket in the dark ocean deeps of Overworld, and these two metaphored deaths had no right to look down on her just because she was a blank. She couldn't help it if pale, featureless flesh barely covered her bony form. Like cat or alligator faces were some great improvement over the smooth cheeks, round eyes, and wide, thin mouths of blanks, the pre-metaphored deaths. Carrying one soul, or a million, didn't require alligator teeth or cat's claws. She knew lots of blanks who worked harder than these two metas.

She decided to let Baast know just how much work she had done and how dirty robes meant more than clean fur and a shaped face forced on a death by humans.

She turned slowly and faced the Egyptian.

Holding her bucket high so the glow of souls illuminated the dark fur and slit green eyes of the meta, she said, "Millions more than you brought to Underworld today."

Baast's eyes widened. Her tail flicked out from under her white robes.

Ammit's great jaws snapped shut.

Littlest Death ignored the cat and the croc. "Every time I go, *millions*. I went into the Marianas Deeps. I often go to high mountain marshes. I go to hospital ventilation shafts. I get dirty, but I bring millions of souls back to the Lake of All Souls."

"Truly, Tiny Death," Ammit said, "the weight of all those souls must be horrific." He slashed his massive tail out and tapped the tip against the bottom of her bucket.

The bucket jumped up.

Baast stepped back to avoid being hit in the face by the bucket.

Littlest Death dropped her robes to get her hand under the bucket to steady it.

The bucket safe once more, she turned her ire on Ammit. "Weighing human souls against feathers isn't real work. One soul? Seriously? That's the best you can do?"

"Yes," Baast hissed. "One human at each trip. That's what many of us do."

Her confident feline smile unnerved Littlest Death.

Stepping forward, Baast forced Littlest Death to back up. "Except in my aspect of war," she hissed.

Too late, Littlest Death remembered that Baast was, in certain Egyptian eras, a war goddess.

The meta cat goddess grew to fill the passage. Her lips lifted, revealing teeth the size of swords. The green glow in her eyes turned from yellow to deepest blood red.

Littlest Death stumbled back another step. Her bucket swayed. The tiny souls sloshed. She fell.

In the moment of fear when she realized the bucket full of tiny sparks would spill all over the black basalt floor, Littlest Death wished she had not let Baast and Ammit catch her off guard and shake her pride in her work. It wasn't like she hadn't run into them and others like them hundreds of times over the last thousand years.

Some were more direct. "When are you going to learn to gather human souls, Littlest Death?" Others, like the truly terrifying and ultimately amazing Ereshkigal of Sumer, were more subtle. "Ah, Littlest Death, to you go the difficult and thankless jobs of an apprentice."

These two just stood around in shadows waiting to make fun of her clothes.

Then, as suddenly as she had tipped, she was upright and steady again.

Baast had caught her and her bucket. The war goddess steadied Littlest, placed the bucket in her hand, and returned to a benign, dark housecat form.

Confused and enraged, Littlest Death gathered herself.

The cat goddess stared at her as if deciding whether to pounce or clean her paws.

Littlest Death said, "I may not be all meta and shaped by the humans like you two," she said, "but I do the job Oldest Death assigned, and I don't interfere with other deaths." She tried to stomp one bony foot, but it caught in her robe and made a smushing sound.

"We all do our assigned jobs," Baast said. "Not even Ammit and I can choose otherwise."

"I have millions of souls to deliver," Littlest Death said. "*Millions.*"

Baast bowed low. "We apologize. We did not understand why Oldest Death gave you the bucket."

Ammit yawned and swished his tail in dismissal.

Flustered by the apology and the bow, Littlest Death stammered a thank you, gathered her robes, and marched away from the two metas.

Behind her, Baast's laughter echoed through the dark stone corridors.

As she marched, Littlest complimented herself for finally getting them to understand how important her job really was. They were so full of themselves just because humans believed in their shapes.

Well, maybe they were deaths long before her. Maybe she was a newcomer and not a meta, but she didn't hide in shadows and scare people into almost spilling precious souls. She did her job. She brought back millions, and they just envied her and her bucket, she told herself.

Oldest Death knew what she did for Underworld, and that's what mattered.

She followed the flow of souls upstream. The stream joined a larger stream, and that stream joined another to become a small river.

The march upslope gave her pride and indignation time to shrink until she could admit to herself that it would still be nice to have a face, to gather humans, and to be one of the bigger deaths.

Secretly, she wanted to bring a human soul back from Overworld—at least once.

Maybe if she did, the other deaths would see her as an equal and understand that her millions were more important than their ones and twos.

Except for Oldest Death, of course. He often brought back thousands and thousands of human souls at once. Some said he could even bring all the souls back from dying distant planets—millions and billions.

Of course, she didn't believe that any more than she believed in the legends of the tree of life and the chalice of transcendence at the bottom of the Lake of All Souls.

Deaths often made up stories. Thousands, and for some millions, of years hauling souls back from Overworld made for boredom, too much time to think, and fertile ground for rumors and tales.

Finally, she found herself on the black stone shores of the Lake of All Souls.

The silver-blue glow of merging, mingling liquid souls in the lake spread away from her as far as she could see. As she gently tipped her bucket and poured the millions of tiny sparks back into the lake from which they had originally come, she wondered just how Oldest Death gathered in a thousand souls per trip.

It had to be a trick like the bucket he had given her. She imagined his scythe was the secret. If she learned his trick, maybe just once she could bring back a couple hundred humans—just to prove she could so the other deaths would leave her alone.

There, on the shores of the Lake of All Souls, Littlest Death came up with a plan.

She'd show them all.

Planning Her Future

The day arrived, and Littlest Death hurried to harvest the tiny souls, the sparks of light dancing in and out of a mass of decaying algae and single-celled organisms accumulating against the upwind shore of a mountain lake. All morning, she'd scuttled about at the edges of Lago Enfermo in the Andes mountains—really, not so much a lake as a puddle in an alpine cirque.

She rushed because she knew that her idol and boss, Oldest Death, would soon head out to perform a huge retrieval of souls. She would follow him—watch him pass out of Underworld. She'd wait a little while then sneak out behind him to see how he managed to gather in so many human souls.

If she were to follow him, observe, and sneak back into Underworld, she'd need time. Her duties would have to be complete before she risked following Oldest Death.

It certainly wouldn't do to get caught following the death born in the making of the universe. No. That would be very bad. Very, very bad.

Someday, she told herself, she'd be like him. She'd go out, scythe in hand, and gather in the living essence of humans felled by famine, plague, pestilence, and war.

Someday.

Distracted by her own fantasy, she tripped on her robe, stumbled over a rock, and nearly spilled her bucket of shining, sloshing, tiny souls.

Splashing through the black, rotting muck and pond scum water, she regained her balance, lifted the hem of her ruined black robes, and steadied her bucket for another dip.

Her job was simple. It had been the same since her beginning, which wasn't really all that long ago if she thought of how many worlds were in the universe and how long some of them had been around and, if she allowed that some of the stories deaths told were true, covered in living things. By death standards, she was still young. If she'd been a live human in Overworld, she'd be maybe thirteen, but time was different in Underworld.

She tried not to think too much about all that.

On a good day, a few hundred years ago, Oldest Death let her gather up the glimmering life energy of a platypus. The experience had been difficult, but she had managed it in the end. Even so, Oldest Death only let her do that once before he sent her back to her normal assignment gathering the sparks of things that had only just barely managed to be alive.

Even if the other planets had lots and lots of life, she worked the Earth. All she had to do was gather up the tiny souls of single-celled creatures, algae, and fungi.

And if she wanted to do it quickly, she'd better pay attention. *Do the job. Focus,* she had to tell herself. *My job is too easy,* she thought. That's why she got distracted. She needed a harder job. Her job was so easy that if she weren't already a death, it would bore her to death.

Paramecia, algae, and fungi are born and die at a furious rate, so Oldest Death gave her the soul-gathering bucket that let her run about the lake scooping up millions of the tiny, sparkly things.

Because there were so many tiny sparks in the world and none of the other deaths dealt with tiny souls, Oldest Death had arranged for Overworld time, Earth time, to sit still for her while she worked.

Tap her bucket rim, time stopped. Tap it again, time started.

She liked that trick. It was another reason she knew she was special. She had heard that some humans worshiped a soul named Santa Claus. She'd never met him, and she wasn't sure he wasn't just another death story, but the tales said he could make time stand still like her. She liked that she might share the time trick with one of the human-revered souls who had been given a face.

Of course, just because time stood still for her in Overworld on Earth didn't mean it stood still in Underworld. She still had to hurry if she wanted to ghost Oldest Death.

Still, the job was too easy, and since the Baast and Ammit incident after her last trip to the Marianas Deeps, she had been thinking a lot about metas. She hated it, but she had started out thinking about how to impress Baast and Ammit. It hadn't taken long for her to envision impressing some of the other deaths who either ignored her or looked down on her.

She gathered her sparks and built up the vision of herself growing into her own robes and standing taller than the other deaths. She would not rise from being Littlest Death to being just a normal death—no, she'd be a meta like Anubis or Chiron or Baast.

No.

She would become Almost Oldest Death and bring thousands of humans back from Overworld in her bucket. She'd be glorious like Ereshkigal.

Wouldn't that be something, to have a whole mythology to back her up while she walked the Overworld and gathered in grateful human souls?

A girl can dream.

Filling her bucket in frozen Earth time, she considered her future as one of the greatest metas ever.

Her visions of greatness turned to the inevitable questions about how she could achieve that greatness, and that, of course, reminded her that she already had a plan and might have wasted her opportunity by daydreaming. A boring job and frozen time made it easy to forget that time in Overworld wasn't connected to time in Underworld.

Focus. Focus. She chastised herself. "Faster," she said aloud.

She hurried to skim the edge of the lake once more, skipping on her unmetaphored, blank boney feet from stone to stone like a human child. She bobbed up and down, dipping her soul bucket into the muck to gather in the millions of itty-bitty sparks she would take through to Underworld and dump into the lake.

She'd deliver the sparks. Then, she'd make her move.

She checked her bucket—not quite full, but full enough, and she had to find Oldest Death before he headed out. She'd learn his trick and get real assignments guiding bright, mature souls—bigger than platypuses—through the veil between worlds and into the Lake of All Souls to commune with all the other souls preparing for their next journey into flesh in Overworld.

Then, the other deaths would respect her. They'd understand how many millions more than them she had handled. If she brought back even one human, they'd see she was a real death. She'd not only bring in buckets full of sparks from bugs, mushrooms, and germs, she'd help human souls evolve, develop, and grow brighter.

Eventually, the humans would know of her. They would bow to her like they bowed to Baast. They would know she was the better death, and they would believe in her so much that they would give her a face.

She sloshed her way out of the muck and water and up toward rock-cast shadows where she restarted time and slipped through a veil into Underworld.

Ereshkigal

Proud of her work and excited for what would come next, Littlest Death held her glowing bucket of souls high with one hand and gathered up her dark robes with the other. Sometimes, stepping through the veil from Overworld to Underworld could be a little tricky—especially if she had to hurry.

Not that she could ever slow down. She was just a hurrying sort of soul. That was another reason the other deaths should respect her. When she became a meta, she'd be the fastest meta ever. She'd probably even have wings like Ereshkigal or Azrael. That would be amazing.

So, she almost leapt into the shadowy spaces. The stone wall melted away and accepted her as what she was, a true denizen of Underworld, the place surrounding all places, the space between spaces, the always and forever that was and will be.

She passed through and landed in warm, musty, misted darkness.

The darkness spoke to her. "Always in a hurry, little one. Always on your way to your next fall."

Littlest Death froze. Expecting more ridicule, she searched the shadows for ambushers.

No. Not ambushers.

She knew the voice in the darkness. It was an old death, a death who would speak to her when others ignored her as not worthy of their time.

It was the winged death, Ereshkigal of Sumer.

Littlest Death lifted her pail of pale souls like a lantern.

The glow fell over Ereshkigal, goddess of the early Mesopotamian vision of Underworld. Seated on a black stone in a black shadow, she smiled. Her bare, bird legs and clawed, hawk's feet dangled from the rock. With her dark wings folded casually behind her, her terrible beauty could not be denied. This was a death goddess many considered to be a monster because the dark gravitas of her office unnerved them. Ereshkigal had seen the rise and fall of civilizations. She had walked among the rising souls released in wars by stone, blade, and bomb.

She might be as old as Oldest Death himself, but Littlest Death was too awed by her to ever ask.

In fact, Littlest Death couldn't quite figure out if Ereshkigal was a friend or just a sadistic spirit who had been too long moving souls from Overworld to the lake.

Ereshkigal often reminded Littlest of the embarrassing moment when, late as usual, Littlest had rushed into the Arena of Duties carrying a bucket full of tiny souls. It had been bad enough she was late to the Arena and that the assignment of new duties had begun without her. To make things worse, she had, in her haste, tripped and spilled the entire bucket full of sparks right at Oldest Death's dark and dangerous feet.

"My robes are high," she said to Ereshkigal. "My bucket is full." Respectfully, Littlest Death did her best to curtsy without spilling her bucket.

Ereshkigal's bird-like, musical laughter danced in the caverns of Underworld. It echoed up the corridors through which the glowing rivers, streams, and rivulets of souls flowed ever outward toward Overworld.

At Littlest's feet, a tiny rivulet of glowing spirit moved outward. It seemed to pause in its flow and press against the narrow banks of its course as if trying to reach toward the source of laughter.

Littlest said, "I fell once two hundred years ago."

"Nothing at all," said Ereshkigal. "A moment. The single heartbeat of a sun."

Recognizing the taunt of an ancient death toward a relatively new death, Littlest did what she always did. She stoically gathered her robes anew and began her dutiful march upstream toward the Lake of All Souls.

Ereshkigal leapt from her rock to the cavern floor. Her leap was a flight of grace and sensual pleasure incarnate.

Littlest Death wanted to feel some sense of pride that this ancient spirit would walk with her, but she knew it would be pointless. Before Ereshkigal left her, there would be pain. It was the price for the attention of the ancient, winged goddess of Sumer. Her people had imagined her into the dark creature she was, and she had no choice but to be what she was.

Littlest hoped that when she had humans who imagined her into a form, she would have the same sense of menace, the same elegance of form, maybe the wings, and certainly the dark, mysterious eyes. It would be so much better than her pale, smooth skin and the sharp bones beneath formless robes.

"A good harvest, Little One?" Ereshkigal asked.

"Millions," Littlest quipped.

"Will you be moving up?"

Littlest quickened her pace. She knew when she was being baited. She'd never admit it, but if Ammit placed her millions of tiny souls on his scale against a single human soul, her bucketful of spirit would amount to nothing at all.

Nothing, and every death in Underworld seemed to know it.

Littlest said, "If Oldest Death sets me a task, that is the task I will do."

Instead of the barb Littlest expected, Ereshkigal said, "Littlest Shade of Underworld, Oldest Death has called us all."

Littlest Death froze. It had been several years since all the deaths had been called to a meeting. Normally, they gathered in groups to get assignments. All the deaths at once meant something important was happening—or about to happen.

"In the Arena?" she asked.

"Yes, Littlest One."

"*You* came to tell me?"

Ereshkigal's wings fluttered a little, as if the idea that she, one of the great deaths, coming as a messenger to Littlest Death might be a bit embarrassing. "I happened to be nearby."

Making sure her cowl covered it, Littlest Death smiled. This was why Littlest Death sometimes thought Ereshkigal might be the only death who didn't completely hate her. Appreciative of the kindness, she said, "Thank you, Great Lady."

Ereshkigal seemed gratified by the formal thanks. "We will gather in the Arena of Duties in two days. Don't be late, but don't be in a hurry again, either." She stretched her wings as if to take flight.

Once her benefactor took flight, Littlest Death would not be able to keep up. "Wait, Lady of the Darkness," she said. "Please tell me."

The dark wings settled, but not so much that Ereshkigal seemed at her ease. "Tell you what, Little One?"

"Assignments? Duties?" She hated to say it. She was afraid to curse her own hopes, but she said, "Changes?"

"Of course, Littlest One. Thus has it always been when he calls us all to the Arena." Ereshkigal spread her wings and flew upstream—probably to her own duties in the past ages and the glory of Sumer.

Watching the glory of Ereshkigal disappear, Littlest Death realized that the Sumerian had left without leaving her trademark pain behind. Ereshkigal was too ancient and experienced to have forgotten, so it must mean something else. Dared she think it might mean respect?

Changes. New duties.

Though the sparks she carried had no weight, the ages of endless, monotonous repetition had become a weight on her heart. Now, suddenly, her bucket seemed lighter.

Littlest moved on upstream.

The rivulet of spirit she followed, shining and silver-blue among the black basalt of Underworld, joined another and widened.

She wanted to be a real death, a meta, a death with wings. Even a cliché scythe like Chronos or Oldest Death would be better than oversized black robes and a bucket.

She forgot Ereshkigal's advice and began to run. She just had to get her bucket to the lake, and she had to follow Oldest Death out into Overworld before the meeting. She would prove she knew how to harvest humans before new duties were assigned.

Emptying the Bucket

Some deaths spoke in low, reverent tones about the endlessness of the Lake of All Souls. Others said it must have an end because rivers of spirit flow outward from it like thousands of fat fingers stretching away from a palm toward the world of light, life, and flesh. If the lake had no end, the death tales went, there could be no shore.

Littlest Death held no opinion on the matter.

She tried to see what was in front of her, which was a basalt rubble-strewn shoreline against which gentle waves of bright, silver-blue liquid lapped. Each living wavelet touched the shore and fell back into the lake.

She knelt next to the lake and carefully tipped the contents of her bucket out and into the glowing liquid soup of souls.

Each tiny spark poured from her bucket, dripped to the surface as a tiny blue-silver ball, skittered across the glowing surface as if momentarily reluctant to join the other souls that made up the liquid of the lake, then flattened out and melted into the greater lake.

Deaths told many tales. Some said a soul melted into the lake was no longer a soul at all. When a bit of soul stuff dripped through into Overworld and inhabited flesh, a new soul was born—fresh and whole.

Others said every soul was a soul—separate but part of the liquid of the lake all at once. The story said the souls all mingled and mixed, learning from one another's lives and gradually flowing toward the flesh again. Eventually they dripped through when and where they chose, and they chose the best life from which to learn and become ever wiser, brighter, and closer to understanding the universe.

Littlest Death didn't know which story was true, but those two she liked best because they meant the sparks she released into the lake were sort of already human souls. They just hadn't learned enough to live in human flesh.

The last of her tiny charges melted into the lake. She sighed and headed for a shadowed and secluded basalt outcropping—her favorite place for hiding from the other deaths and peering out over the placid, glowing surface toward the center of the lake. There, legends said, the pure heart of all things beat in the deeps.

Alone, hidden, and listening to the quiet lapping of souls on the shore, she could let go of the indignity of her duties and her position as the last death born into Underworld.

She settled her bucket in the shadows and considered climbing up onto her perch atop the rock and resting for a while, but that would mean giving up on her plan to find Oldest Death and follow him.

She had to learn if she wanted to grow, and she had to grow if she wanted to change her duties in Underworld.

She turned from her rest, from the silver heart of the lake, and from her hidden bucket. Keeping to shadows, she stole away toward the River Styx, which was where she believed she would find Oldest Death.

Greek Tragedy

While sneaking from shadow to shadow, Littlest tried to imagine what her meta name would be. She knew the metas got their names from the dreams, hopes, and fears of humans—at least that's what she'd been told.

Ereshkigal was the name given the winged death who sometimes spoke kindly to her, but it was given by the tribes of humans who imagined Ereshkigal's form. Those humans saw her as a hawk that came in the night from on high— silently swooping down and ripping the soul from the body with talons. She hoped her humans would respect her but not be quite so afraid of her.

Oldest Death had no name except Oldest Death. While greatest and oldest of them all, he was no larger in any visible sense. Well, he was larger than Littlest. His scythe was three times taller than Littlest with her cowl up, but he was not as tall as Ereshkigal nor as tall as Ammit was long. Oldest Death was a bit taller than Isis or a Valkyrie or any of the named angels like Azrael.

While taller than Littlest, he was in some ways more like her than any of the other deaths.

He wore similar black robes—the same pitiless black as the dark stones of Underworld. Oldest's robes fell to ankle-length like hers would if she grew a little.

Her face was blank. His was mostly blank.

Well, at least his was a human skull, but it might as well have been blank because he rarely let it appear from behind his cowl. Most of the time, the darkness inside his cowl was the only face anyone or any death ever saw.

No. Humans hadn't named him. He was only called Oldest Death because he was first. She thought it was a little unfair that just because he was first, Oldest Death told her and all the others what their duties would be. His being oldest was just an accident of the universe.

So, maybe he wasn't greatest. Maybe they just all thought he was. Maybe all the deaths had believed him into being their boss.

No. That wasn't true. She knew that.

She was sneaking away to watch him because he was special. She'd have no reason to follow him if he weren't.

When Oldest Death walked the physical worlds, he swung his great scythe and gathered thousands of fully grown, conscious human souls into the folds of his robes.

Thousands.

Some deaths said he had even gathered millions or billions when asteroids hit the Earth or he travelled to other worlds where stars exploded or pride and greed destroyed whole species.

If such tale-tellers were to be believed, which she doubted, Oldest Death gathered souls from the Overworld of other worlds—maybe even all of them.

Littlest only worked Earth.

All the deaths Littlest knew only worked Earth, but she had heard that on the far side of the lake other deaths gathered souls from other worlds. She had also heard that when a sun expanded to consume a world, Oldest Death was there to gather in the lost and bring them safely to the lake.

When plague broke out and swept across a world, ending the highest forms on that world, Oldest Death was the one who attended the souls in transition.

When the Earth was covered in great wars, Oldest Death stood at the center, beckoning to all the bright lights lifted from the flesh and seeking a new path toward what they could become.

She had heard such tales, but she had never seen him do any of those things. She had, however, once seen him open his robes and release several hundred souls into the lake. They fell from the shadows of his robe the way the tiny sparks fell from her bucket.

Some lingered in human form for a moment, wraiths walking upon the surface of the lake, before slowly melting into the spirit waters.

The scythe and robe trick was what she needed to learn. That's why she followed him.

She stole along a river of spirit into a long cavern leading toward ancient Greece. There, the humans had named the river of souls for a warrior goddess, Styx, who had battled the Titans.

Littlest found Oldest flowing like a midnight cloud shadow across the stony floor. He travelled quickly and silently, following the serpentine Styx outward from the Lake of All Souls and toward the inevitable gateway into the world of light, life, and the living.

She took care to hold to deepest darks to avoid his attention. Certainly, she had travelled such routes many times, but she found herself sucking in hot, sulfurous air as if she needed to breathe like a human child running to keep up with a thoughtless parent.

She was, after all, a death, so she told herself how ridiculous that was. She didn't need to breathe.

Once, five hundred years ago and before she spilled her bucket of sparks at his feet, Oldest Death assigned her two desert kangaroo rats, a collared lizard, and a male platypus. Right there in the Arena of Duties in front every death, she had asked for a rat scythe because Ammit had told her that in some worlds even deaths who took rats carried scythes.

The laughter had been thunderous.

She had breathed then, too. That only made the laughter louder.

Oldest Death had silenced the arena with a single sweep of his hand before he sent her on her way.

Followed by laughter, she had shuffled out of the arena, dragging her bucket behind her.

Still, she did her job.

The rats had been rats and glad to be out of the flesh and on to the afterlife. One had been crushed by a rock slide that destroyed her newly finished nest. The other had been eaten by a snake.

No problems there.

The collared lizard, though less excited about being out of the flesh, was at least pragmatic enough to understand there was no going back to the body a hawk had torn up.

The platypus, however, was not at all happy about being dead.

It struggled to go back to its mate and its two little platypups. It had a nice little clear-water pool full of crustaceans and gravel worms. That platypus knew it had a good thing going, and it did not want to leave the flesh even though its body had been cut in half by a crocodile.

Littlest Death had to spend nearly half a day sitting beside the pool while the Platypus tried to get back into the front half of the body the croc had left. Half a day of waiting without freezing time was not how most deaths would have handled it, but back then she had thought she couldn't take the little soul unless it wanted to go. She had believed she had to wait. She didn't want to be laughed at again, so she was laughed at again.

Hundreds of years later, a few deaths still made fun of her.

Most, however, had moved on to crueler jokes after she spilled the bucket full of sparks on the bony feet of Oldest Death.

Since the spill, she hadn't even seen a platypus. Except for that one long-ago trip into Overworld for larger souls, her job had been bacteria, fungi, and paramecia since her earliest memory.

She'd change that.

Littlest Death tucked herself in behind a ridge of ancient basalt. She pressed herself into the shadows made by the silver glow of the river of souls and the dark stone shielding her from Oldest Death.

Given how far she had followed Oldest and how many times the river Styx had split, Littlest was sure they must be getting near to the veil separating Underworld from Overworld.

She knew Styx had a guardian, so she'd have to be careful.

Most of the larger flows of souls into Overworld were served by metas, and those flows often had guardians.

Littlest didn't know why. Guardians weren't deaths. Humans made them up. They weren't important, so she hadn't given them much thought.

When enough humans agreed about some afterlife thing they made up, it happened in Underworld. That's how metas got faces and wings and claws and teeth and such. If enough humans agreed a giant salamander guarded the entrance to the afterlife, a giant salamander took up residence on the river of souls that fed the flesh in that region of Overworld.

The Greeks had several guardians. One was the warrior goddess Styx, but she was usually the river itself. Once, Littlest had met Charon. He was like Ereshkigal in that he occasionally talked to Littlest, but he was even harder to read than Ereshkigal.

Littlest had spent time around some of the others, too.

The Mayan trickster guardian, Yum Cimil, was actually fun. More than most Underworld denizens, he had a sense of humor. He was both a guardian and a death. In a huge cavern near a Yucatecan cenote veil between Underworld and Overworld, he kept a constant raucous party of souls going. It was one of only a few places in Underworld where music could be heard, where dancing took place, and where the souls spent time together before entering the lake.

She had liked Yum Cimil's cavern for a while—until she realized his sense of humor had a very nasty edge to it.

Later, Ereshkigal, laughing at Littlest Death as usual, told her the humans had imagined Yum Cimil into a special kind of guardian whose job was to keep them from returning to the Lake of All Souls.

That explained the party.

Suddenly, Oldest Death stopped.

Littlest froze and focused her thoughts on hiding from her quarry. She wondered how many souls Oldest would bring back.

Maybe Earth was having a plague.

Maybe a huge war.

Maybe—just maybe because she probably would have heard about it since it was ancient Greece—Earth had been hit by a small asteroid.

Pressing her back to cold stone, she thought maybe she should start breathing just so she could hold her breath.

Peeking carefully around the sharp edge of her hiding place, she watched Oldest Death reach out one dark-robed arm.

At the opposite wall of the cavern, a huge shadow separated itself from the darkness. At first, she thought a boulder of basalt had come loose under Oldest Death's touch, but the boulder stood up on four black legs and the giant form moved toward Oldest Death and into the light of the stream of souls.

Kerberos, the three-headed hell hound of Hades, loomed over Oldest Death. The animal's massive shoulders and heads almost scraped against the cavern ceiling.

Oldest Death reached up. His robe sleeve fell back from his bony hand, and he dug the points of his fingers into the fur beneath Kerberos's right-head ear.

The monstrous dog's broad chest heaved. All three heads chuffed as one. Its right, rear leg thumped against the stone floor in sympathetic response to the scratching. The other two heads whimpered, tilted, and rolled as if they too were being scratched.

This, Littlest Death thought, *was the vicious, monstrous, three-headed guardian dog of Hades?* Clearly, the Greeks didn't have the dark, poetic souls she had been told they had. This thing was a lap dog.

Okay, the lap dog was easily five times the size of Littlest. The monster hound was black as death, and its three heads all suffered from too many teeth and an inability to keep from drooling all over the rocks of the cavern.

Oldest Death stopped scratching.

The dog stopped whimpering and thumping.

Oldest Death turned toward her.

She ducked back into cover. If he caught her, it would be the end of her—or worse. She had once heard tell of a meta called Komet who neglected her duties and been sentenced to hand-carry single tiny, tiny soul sparks to barren worlds in an attempt to get new life started. That would be much worse than being Littlest Death hauling buckets of sparks for millennium after millennium.

Focused on hiding from Oldest and the hound, Littlest had been ignoring the shadows upstream. Behind her, a pebble clattered in the darkness.

Startled, she almost jumped out of the shadows.

Settling back into hiding, she peered into the darkness along the upslope stone wall.

Something moved in the shadows there.

She supposed Oldest Death might have brought another death along—maybe Hades. She'd never heard of Oldest Death doing such a thing, but she wasn't so prideful as to believe what she had heard was all that could be known about Oldest Death. He'd been in Underworld since the universal heart pulsed for the first time and the uniform sea of quarks congealed and conformed to the physical laws and limitations of Overworld.

She shrank more deeply into shadow, and she tried to will her robes to become darker and her thoughts to become smaller.

Again, the something moved in the darkness.

She tried to remember Greek stories. Whatever was moving in the shadows probably fit their visions.

Heroes. Greeks like heroes who sneak in and out of Underworld.

It could be a Hero. She'd never seen a Hero, and they sometimes slipped by Kerberos.

Wasn't Theseus supposed to have tricked the dog? Or was that Heracles? Pirithous? She wasn't sure who that one was, but his name came to mind, so she must have heard a story about him.

What she was sure of was that Greeks went in and out of Underworld like they had private doors from their lives. Sometimes, they used food to trick the dog. Sometimes, they had to fight him.

The way Oldest Death and the dog were getting along, she was beginning to understand how the Greeks could move in and out of Underworld so easily. All three heads of the monster were pushovers. A little scratch behind one ear, and they were all drooling puddles of pleasure.

She hoped the movement in the shadows was a loose soul. Maybe one of the other deaths screwed up and a soul had gotten loose.

Greeks didn't always stay dead. Sometimes, they snuck back into Overworld. Ereshkigal had told Littlest stories about Greek shades, but she thought shades were the same as souls—weren't they? Maybe this one escaped before it was returned to the lake. That would be nice. Maybe all the deaths would ridicule someone else and forget her epic incident of the spilled bucket.

Then, she remembered that Greeks had demigods—and maybe demons?

The thing moved again.

Could be a demon, she thought.

If Greeks could dream up the three-headed dog, they could put all kinds of other things along their river of souls. She wasn't sure the Greeks had demons, but lots of cultures did. Greeks probably did, too. It could be one of those.

If it was a shade, maybe she'd be able to gather it in and take it back to the lake. That might even convince Oldest Death she could be trusted.

She had just about convinced herself the something was a soul she should catch and haul back to the Lake of All Souls when Kerberos let out a cavern shaking, three-headed howl.

Gravel and dust fell from the ceiling. The placid, glowing silver-blue waters of the river of souls rippled and danced.

In spite of her shaking, Littlest Death chanced a peek around the rocks.

In the Greek vision of the passage from one world to the next, an actual marble arch supported on ancient Doric capitals above smooth pillars separated the cavern darkness from the light of the living world.

Oldest Death touched one pillar.

Brilliant blue light flashed and filled the space beyond. Where there had been shadow and emptiness, a great lake of clear water now spread out under cerulean skies and feathered clouds. Verdant rolling hills in the distance shimmered as breezes swept over succulent grasses. A fresh, poppy-scented breeze blew into Underworld between the pillars.

She had heard of the Elysian Fields, a place of heroes between Underworld and Overworld, but she had never dared believe it was so beautiful. Littlest Death clutched at the neck of her robes.

Oldest Death stepped over a low mound of stone, lifted a pole from near his feet, and pressed it downward. As if rising to the surface of the stone cavern floor, a long, low boat rose around him until he stood in its center, his pole poised to press the boat forward. As if floating on stone were the same as floating on water, the boat slipped through the rock, past the archway, and outward onto the idyllic lake.

Charon, then, Littlest thought. Oldest Death was taking Charon's boat on his way to some Greek tragedy. And, he was going through the Elysian Fields before he entered Overworld.

She wanted to follow him, but she hadn't planned on the boat or the dog.

Unless she jumped on his boat, she couldn't follow him through the Elysian Fields.

She told herself the boat was too small for him to bring back an epic number of shades.

Okay, maybe it would only be hundreds on the boat. Certainly, she could learn something from that. She shook with envy.

Only a few deaths were honored to bring back hundreds of souls at a time. Oldest Death was the oldest and most important among them, and when he went to Overworld, he rarely came back carrying less than a thousand souls. Pestilence, plague, war, natural disaster—those were the things that drew Oldest Death out of Underworld.

But, she didn't have a boat.

She told herself it didn't matter—that Oldest wasn't going to gather in thousands and thousands anyway. The boat was too small for that many Greek shades, and if he put all the souls in his robe she wouldn't see much.

Of course, she knew nobody knew how many souls he could fit in his robes, but it felt good to blame the size of the boat for the fact that she wasn't going to learn his thousands of souls trick.

She tightened in her crouch for a dash to the boat.

The monstrous canine guardian barked once—a thundering three-toned explosion of sound.

The three-headed dog was huge and not just a decoration.

Then, there was the thing in the shadows.

She settled back, turned, and pressed her back to the rock that hid her. Disappointment and maybe a little relief washed over her.

After a few moments, she peeked around the edge of the rock.

The Center head and the Right head of the hellhound watched Oldest Death floating away. Left head, however, seemed intent on her hiding place. She couldn't tell if it was looking for her or for the thing in the shadows. From Kerberos's perspective, they had to be in the same line of sight.

Then, it was too late to follow. The beauty framed by the archway disappeared. Only black stone remained. Oldest Death was gone.

Defeated, she shrank down into the shadows behind her hiding stone.

She had wanted so badly to learn, to understand, to know how he could gather in thousands of human souls at a time.

She had dared to believe if she could learn that trick, the other deaths wouldn't laugh at her anymore. Maybe even Baast would lose her condescending tone. Littlest Death had even hoped that if she could prove she could carry just one human soul, Oldest Death might assign her to human soul duty.

One soul. It was all she really needed.

She had waited a thousand years. One skill she knew she had was patience. She'd try again—a less doggy and watery route.

She'd be discreet. She'd wait a few decades or so. There was no point in drawing attention to herself.

The something in the darkness moved again, and Littlest Death decided there might still be a chance for her.

If the something *was* a loose human soul and she gathered it in …

No. Oldest Death wasn't stupid. If she gathered a wayward soul here, he'd know she'd been watching him.

Maybe she could hide it for a while—maybe a couple hundred years.

Gravel scrabbled. A huffing, breathing noise came from the shadows.

Kerberos answered. His rumbling, three-toned chuff shook dust from the walls.

Not good.

If the big dog investigated, she'd be caught, and she couldn't choke that monster like Heracles had.

That was right!

She remembered one of the stories. Heracles had choked Kerberos with a lion skin or a wooden club or something.

She didn't have a lion skin or a wooden club, and the only something was the something in the shadows.

Littlest decided it would be best if she headed back upstream toward the Lake of All Souls. She'd get her bucket and hide what she had done by doubling up on her assigned work.

Careful to be silent and as shadowy as she could be, she slipped away upstream.

Several times, a scuff or scrabble behind her pulled her up short.

Each time she froze, she told herself it was nothing, but part of her knew it was something because the sound worried her. The something was following her. Each time she heard it, she slipped deeper into shadows and watched the trail along the glowing stream for movement. Each time, she saw nothing.

When Littlest was sure she had left the arch, the dog, and the Elysian Fields all behind her, she stepped out of the shadows and headed toward her favorite sitting place on the banks of the Lake of All Souls.

To throw off any suspicion, she held her shoulders high and strode with purpose. She'd seen Osiris walk like that. He was important, and he knew it. She could be important if she wanted to be, so she walked as if she had an important task to accomplish.

Even once she was out of the Greek metaphor and walking the well-lit paths beside the large soul rivers—and even when she had come all the way back to the lake, she had the creepy feeling something not quite fully dead still followed her.

Ditching the Dog

The feeling that the something dogged her continued all the way to the lake, but every time she looked back, she only saw dark shadows and glowing soul rivers. When she reached the shores of the lake, she relaxed enough to look out over the lake and consider her future fending off disrespect, carrying her bucket, and filling it with tiny sparks.

The something chose that moment to attack.

From behind, a three-toned yapping and the scrabble of basalt gravel startled her. She turned to face her attacker.

A black, three-headed puppy the size of a full-grown Rottweiler bounded out from behind a boulder, galloped toward her, and leapt on her before she even understood what it was. The thing knocked her to the ground. Her robes flew up and tangled her legs and one of her arms. Sharp gravel ground into her back, and she closed her eyes under the onslaught.

Flailing her free hand to try and fend off the animal, she realized she had been followed by some perversion of the story of the Greek guardian, Kerberos. The monster dog of Hades had a puppy.

The thing danced around, over, and on her chest. Three tongues licked at her face and soaked her cowl and robes.

Littlest Death rolled back and forth, trying to dislodge the thing.

Eventually, the pouncing, prancing, playful monster backed off and she sat up.

Three fire-eyed blockheads stared at her, tongues lolling.

"What in Hades are you?" she asked.

Center Head cocked. Left yapped. Right blinked and panted.

Littlest Death got to her feet and backed away.

The Six-eyed Demon Dog bounced up onto all fours and took a tentative step to follow.

"No!" Littlest commanded. "Go home!"

Left Head's ears drooped. His nose pointed to the ground.

Center cocked the other way. The flop of his half-upright ears flipped to the other side.

Right shook as if a flea had bitten him behind the ear.

Littlest backed away a few more paces. She backed into a hip-high boulder and sidled around it until it separated them.

The animal took another step to follow.

Littlest Death picked up a stone and threw it at the head in the middle.

The stone flew over the Tartarusian Taunter's heads and back along the edge of the Lake of All Souls. It clattered to the ground, bounced, rolled, and came to a stop.

Left Head turned hard over its shoulder and marked the final resting place of the stone. Center yipped his satisfaction. Right twisted back to look for the stone.

Suddenly, as if all three heads had come to a silent agreement, the Puppy of Pouncing jumped up, twisted in the air, and bolted off in pursuit of the stone.

Littlest Death ran for her bucket and the nearest veil. If she could get to a veil, she didn't think the whelp of a guardian would be able to follow her.

The ruse almost worked. Littlest Death escaped into Overworld. She even managed to fill her bucket. Feeling almost normal, she returned.

She stepped through the veil, and there was the hound, sitting just inside the veil—waiting, the thrown stone in Left's mouth. Center and Right peered at her from sad eyes as if apologizing for their failure to retrieve the tossed rock.

A day and a dozen attempts to ditch the dog later, she understood it had been a mistake to try and run away from the puppy. The Three-Headed Damnation had thought her dodge-and-dash a game.

It had given chase.

The damned thing was a nuisance. It was just adding to her misery by giving the other deaths another reason to laugh at her.

Even Ereshkigal, whom she occasionally thought of as a friend, had called her Puppy Death as the pair of them had dashed past the elder goddess. The only one who had seen them and hadn't laughed at her was Anubis, but she knew what the Jackal-headed Egyptian was thinking. He didn't like any other dog heads in Underworld, so he gave her a damning glare like somehow the puppy chasing her around was her fault.

At least Oldest Death just ignored her the same way he normally had for the last thousand years.

The chase ended while she had been running along the edges of the Lake of All Souls in the deepest caverns of Underworld. She needed to escape the thing, empty her bucket, and get to the Arena of Duties. Being late again wasn't an option.

Exhausted, she tripped on her dark robes, leapt, twisted, and scuttled to catch her balance before stumbling and skidding to a halt. Somehow, she managed to keep her bucket from spilling.

The puppy loped. It capered. It spun in excitement. The thing never seemed to tire.

She tried to hurry on, but two of the puppy heads, Left and Center, caught her trailing robe in their teeth. The third one, Right, yelped in joy.

She stumbled and wondered what perverse human minds had imagined such an abomination into existence.

One hand protected her bucket while she clutched at her robe with the other and tugged.

They liked that. It seemed like everything she tried just made the thing like her more.

She had once heard a living woman yell at her dog. The dog was tearing at a dying rabbit. Littlest Death had been gathering fungus sparks in a nearby woods, and she went to investigate.

The rabbit was happy to leave its flesh. It had popped out and come to her while the dog molested its body. Littlest Death had been proud for a moment because she thought she'd get to retrieve a rabbit. At that time, a rabbit would have been the largest soul Littlest Death had ever fetched.

However, The Wild Hunt had come for the Rabbit. They were very unhappy to find Littlest Death lifting their rabbit soul, and they made it known by riding their stags right over her.

The human woman had screamed "Leave it!" over and over to get the dog let the rabbit's body alone.

Making use of her memory, Littlest Death yanked at her robes again and screamed, "Leave it!"

The dog hadn't listened to the woman.

The Triptych of Terror didn't listen either.

Littlest Death fell. Protecting the bucket kept her from protecting herself. She hit cowl-first, face against the dark, lava rock floor.

Kerberwhelp pounced on her back. Oversized puppy paws danced up her back and over her shoulders.

She managed to keep the bucket out of the chaos of his dance, push up to one elbow, and lift her head. She searched for an escape path.

Too late. Three gleeful, floppy-eared, hell-hound faces grinned and bathed her in sulfurous saliva.

"Stop!" she yelled, twisting her face back and forth—first from one lapping tongue and then from another. "Go away!" She slapped at the bobbing, slobbering puppy heads.

It was so unfair that the Hades hound had three heads and she only had one free hand. Her other hand still gripped her precious bucket, and she dared not break the grip or hit the puppy.

She wasn't sure how the puppy worked. It might have a soul, and smacking the bucket against a head might harvest that soul and kill the pup. It might not have a soul, and a head smack might only dent the bucket and spill the sparks.

What she was sure of was that full deaths simply did not go around bucket-beating puppies. Hitting puppies would get her the wrong kind of attention whether they had souls or not. She couldn't imagine being laughed at and judged for puppy abuse.

Quietly, she tried reasoning. "I have to go." She bunched her knees up under her. "I have work."

The slapping-tongued puppy heads weaved and bobbed, but the onslaught of playfulness subsided a little.

She crawled to the shore, squinting through slobber. There, the dog danced around her back but not into the silvery souls. Carefully, still fighting the Robe-tugging Tumult, she tipped her sparks safely into the lake.

Free to use both hands, she freed her robes, got up onto her knees, and managed to carefully push against the broad chest of the pup.

All three heads sniffed at her hand. Right licked it.

She got to her feet once more. She said, "Good puppies. That's a good dog."

She picked up a bit of obsidian and tossed it onto a nearby rubble pile.

Two of the heads were fooled, and that was enough. The third head, Center, still watched her longingly, but two heads are better than one, and Center was reluctantly dragged along by Right and Left as they directed their shared, soot-black doggy body toward the tossed stone.

Littlest Death gathered up the loose billows of her robe and ran with all her heart. If she hurried, she might, maybe, just maybe, make it to The Arena of Duties in time for assignments. She couldn't be late again. She'd never live it down.

Besides, this could be the moment, finally, when she graduated from one-celled organisms to evolving, thinking, feeling people.

New Assignments

Death tales and rumors said the Arena of Duties had once been called the Cavern of Duties long before Littlest Death existed. She didn't understand why it might have been called a cavern. It wasn't so much a cavern or even an arena as it was an amphitheater. Curved, concentric tiers of thousands of seats rose upward from a center dais.

It might have been a cavern once, she supposed. Maybe Oldest Death willed that it be a more ordered and austere place and gave it much better dual-sun overhead lighting.

Littlest Death hadn't been around then. That had been like a bazillion, gazillion years ago.

She hated that she had been the newest death for a thousand years and the other deaths more-or-less ignored her.

No. That wasn't quite true.

Ignoring her was bad but manageable. When they didn't ignore her, it was much worse. She could feel them looking down on her. Some even taunted her, which she didn't think they were supposed to do, but Oldest Death hadn't ever really stopped them, and she couldn't stop them.

Breathless, which was pretty normal since she didn't have to breathe at all, she skittered into the Arena of Duties, made herself as small as she could, and walked up a corridor between seating sections to the curved front row of seats.

Only a few of the assembled deaths showed any sign of noticing her. Most were already focused on Oldest Death on the dais at the focal point of the arena. He was speaking, of course. That's what he did. He either ignored them or told them stuff.

Not for the first time, she wondered why being the first death meant he was in charge forever.

Bucket in hand, she turned her back on him and tried to climb the steps up into the heights of the amphitheater, hoping to hide in the back rows, the highest rows—already despairing that she would not be assigned new duties because she was late. She certainly wouldn't get a human soul. She doubted she'd even get a salamander or a cricket. It would be back to single-cells and fungi for her. She might as well have stayed out gathering sparks.

That stupid puppy had made her late, and now she was going to get the tiny death assignments she always got.

Ereshkigal had once taunted her by saying, "If a death can't be punctual, how can she be trusted to carry souls that matter?"

One of the deaths on an aisle seat hissed at her as she passed, "Spiller." Another muttered something that sounded like, "Late, Rookie."

She had learned to ignore such things.

She found and took a seat between two empties. As she sat down, Oldest Death finished the opening litany of origins. "In the first breath, the gift of life came forth from the heart of the universe. In the second breath came forth death, and death brought the value of life, hope, and compassion. From our sacred duty is born growth and learning. From our birth to our final trip to the Overworld, we serve as we were made."

Deaths don't applaud, but if they did they would have. Oldest Death was *the* death that came forth on the second breath of the universe. The rest of the assembled deaths all came later, as life multiplied, diversified, and spread out—as it was made to do.

The litany always made Littlest Death painfully aware she was the last death—the most recent death. She hoped a new death would appear soon—one younger, smaller, and newer than her. There hadn't been a need yet, and as far as she knew, she was and would always be the youngest death. She was and would always be the death who brings back the tiny sparks.

But there had been the two kangaroo rats, the lizard, and that one platypus.

That had been a good day.

If there had been one good day, there could be another.

As Oldest Death made the assignments, each death rose and left the arena, intent on seeking out their assigned rivulet of souls, following it to its entry into Overworld, and retrieving the soul or souls assigned.

Of course, the meta deaths, the ones like Anubis, Ammit, Ereshkigal, Shatan, Yama, and the oh-too-many righteous angels, all kept their normal assignments. They all rose pretty much as one and headed back to their respective gates, arches, and caverns.

Little-by-little, the seats emptied.

Little-by-little, it became harder and harder to shrink into her robes and hide.

Where she had been sitting between two empty seats, she now sat in an entirely empty section of the amphitheater. She knew her dark robes made her like a black stone on an empty white beach.

Oldest Death always handled the biggest jobs himself. He would be handling war, pestilence, and famine, as usual. He assigned terrorist attacks, regional disease outbreaks, and natural disasters to some of the more accomplished blank deaths. He assigned souls to meta deaths and their minions by continent, region, and belief. Next, he assigned the one-offs, the individuals who were not part of a belief system or who were so outcast they had given up on all beliefs. At the very last, he assigned the children who had not lived long enough to know what a lifetime might be like. Innocence had no need of metaphors and illusions. Young, dying children often went to a single, blank death because child lives were too short to learn the beliefs and metaphors adults created to soften the transition of the spirit from the body.

Eventually, he got around to assigning higher animals—the creatures of thought and feeling, like whales, horses, dolphins, dogs, cats, octopi, ravens, and pigs.

When the auditorium had completely emptied except for her and Oldest Death, he peered up over the empty seats at her and spoke. He neither accused nor attacked. He just stated the fact. “Late again.”

Ashamed, she nodded.

“You know what you have to do, right? Or, do you need me to make the formal assignment.”

Dejectedly, she said, “No, Sir. I know.”

He nodded, picked up his staff—the staff that was sometimes a scythe. It gleamed under the overhead pocket suns that made up the lighting of the Arena of Duties. For a moment, she thought she saw the fabled blade flash in the light.

Some said only humans saw the blade and it meant Oldest Death had come for them.

Ereshkigal had once said the blade, if it appeared, was so sharp the cutting edge was invisible and would cut life from flesh before you could see the blade touch the cord holding the soul to the body.

Seeing the gleam in the sunlight, she could almost believe it.

Then, the blade was gone and Oldest Death leaned on his staff. His robes absorbed all light. A shadow inside a shadow no matter how much light filled the cavern, Oldest Death was the absence of light.

He turned his back on her, and she knew he would be gone in moment. She spoke up.

"Sir," she managed.

He paused, but he did not turn.

"Sir," she began again. "Might there be a bigger soul—not human but a little bigger than my bucket—I could bring back?"

He turned, and she peered into the darkness inside his hood.

"Not a big soul," she stammered on. "A little one. Just a—"

He interrupted her. "Like the platypus?"

She had hoped he wouldn't bring that up. She forced herself to face him and not turn away. "I'm better, now, Sir. I've done millions of souls in a single bucket."

He remained stillness and shadows.

She felt him through her whole ethereal body. Just as his robes were the black absence of light, his gaze was the frozen vacuum of the shadows between stars.

She had his attention, now. She had nothing to lose except a million years of bucket work. "I can be more assertive," she said. "I was hoping for—"

A cutting gesture with his staff shut her up. He said, "You were hoping for an advanced soul? A sentient? Perhaps a human?"

Suddenly embarrassed she had asked, she pretended she had not. She stood and shuffled down the aisle stairs. It was time to go and do what she always ended up doing and would likely always do. There were germs and fungi to reap.

Unfortunately, walking down the stairs brought her closer to the dais, and he gave her his undivided attention every step of the way.

One thing no creature, living or dead in Overworld or Underworld, ever wants is the undivided attention of the most ancient of all darknesses, Oldest Death.

She was almost ready to scream when she reached the final step before she could turn away and run for the safety of her secret place near the Lake of All Souls.

Oldest Death interrupted her desperate desire to escape by saying, "I do have a special assignment for you."

She froze. She clutched at the neck of her robes and pretended she didn't feel the fear and hope growing in her chest. *Special assignment* could mean so many things.

"I want you to make very sure every single single-celled organism in and near a hospital room has been reaped and returned to the lake." He handed her an assignment order—an actual, physical work order sheet containing instructions.

She'd never seen such a thing before. She took it, read it, and understood she would be going to a 21st Century American hospital room.

A children's ward—the absolute worst.

She would be near souls in need, and she would be gathering only the tiniest souls to fill her bucket.

"Maybe," she whispered.

"Yes?"

She spoke up, trying to be clear, confident, and hopeful. "Maybe while I'm there, I could bring back a child?" It sounded to her like a question rather than the offer she had intended it to be.

"I would rather you didn't," Oldest Death said. "But if there is one, you may." Then, he was gone—probably off to harvest a few thousand souls at a go from some global epidemic.

Alone, she stood in the amphitheater. As if she were a pitcher and warm water were being poured slowly into her, she filled with joy and relief. Then, the water cooled. Soon, she was full of new fears she had not considered before.

She didn't want to consider fears. Not now. Not when she had just been promoted—even if it had been a backhanded promotion.

She willed her legs to move, tripped on her robes, gathered them up, and pushed out into the caverns and corridors of Underworld. She left the Arena of Duties behind. The bright light of the pocket suns gave way to the chilled silver-blue light emanating from the rivers, rivulets, and pools that flowed outward from the Lake of All Souls.

The Weird Whelp sat outside the arena, waiting, wagging his dark tail so it made a thumpity-thump sound against black stone.

She took Center between her hands and kissed him on the nose, which set Left and Right to jealous lapping at her cheeks. "I'm going to get a soul!" she said. "A real soul! I'll be just like the other deaths."

Tossing Stones

Her excitement and fear battled until she reached the Lake of All Souls on the way to the river of spirit to 21st Century, predominately Lutheran, North Central Ohio. At the river root where the lake poured out into the flow of souls to Overworld, she stopped.

The Kerberwhelp danced around her, excited that perhaps a playful moment was at hand.

She shook her head and said, "Stupid—" She stopped. She'd been about to call the dog Kerberwhelp, but she realized that wouldn't do. Since she didn't seem to be able to get rid of it, she'd have to find a real name for it—one that fit it.

She tried a new one. "Stupid Death Puppy."

No. She'd work on it.

Looking about, she realized they stood near the place where she often dumped her bucket and where she hid from the other deaths to think.

She turned her back on the cavorting Dark Dog and paced along the shore.

A real soul. A human. If there was one, she could bring it back.

But if there wasn't one, she was just on another errand of spark gathering. Sure, she'd bring in a million souls from the hospital. That was better than just one, so she told herself it would still be a good trip.

She didn't believe herself. Something had happened to her. Just a few days ago, she would have believed herself.

Baast and Ammit.

Everything had been fine before she ran into them.

No. It hadn't all been fine.

They just pushed her over the edge—them, and the dog, and Ereshkigal, and hiding from Oldest Death next to the River Styx.

Littlest tried to focus on her work—on the task in front of her.

She'd been to hospitals before. They were nasty places when it came to the death of tiny things. The whole building and every human in it worked to destroy single-celled lives. More than any other place, she had to stop time in a hospital if she wanted to do a good job.

A human, though. That was different. Deaths didn't stop time for human souls. It wasn't done. It wasn't like dipping the bucket to pick up a hundred thousand sparks at a time. She would actually touch the soul—reach out and take its hand.

There would be other human souls coming and going in a hospital—not like a battlefield where everyone was leaving. In a hospital, souls often arrived faster than they left.

She'd never really had to think about the coming and going before. Once she stopped time, all the coming and going of large souls became part of the background, like a painting she might walk by or a song playing while she wafted through a building on the way to a park pond or a city sewer system.

She'd wanted this moment for like a gadtrillion years, and now that it might be here she wasn't sure she could do it—wasn't sure how to do it.

At the worst, it'll be like the platypus, she told herself. Sometimes, humans didn't want to leave. She had heard that sometimes they wouldn't leave and didn't. She thought Ammit had told her that. It might have been Anubis. She was pretty sure it was an Egyptian.

How would she handle it if her human wouldn't leave? Nobody had told her that.

The important thing was to relax. Odds were, there'd be no human soul to bring back anyway. Oldest had made that pretty clear.

Littlest Death had been wandering along the shores of the lake while she worried the possible and unlikely in her mind. When she looked up and took in her surroundings, she found herself next to her sitting rock, and she settled down for a think.

Oldest Death wouldn't have mentioned a human soul unless …

Toes digging into the cold, dark sand of the lakeshore, she considered what she hoped she was about to do—the life that was about to end and the soul she would bring to the lake.

Quickly bored by her obviously flawed choice to sit and think, the Three-headed Monster turned in circles, once for each head, and plopped down for a nap.

All souls came from the lake and returned to the lake. All life began and ended there. Older deaths called the Lake of All Souls the alpha and omega of Underworld.

Once upon a time, the lake was no more than a hollow place in the dark stone of Underworld, but on that first day, that day of the first breath, the universe had manifested a branch of the tree of life at the very center of the emptiness. Cradled in the hand-like twigs at the end, the branch held the chalice from which life overflows.

Thus, the Lake of All Souls filled from the overflow of the chalice.

Even Littlest Death knew it was an illusion—a mythic image created by the deaths for the deaths. She supposed even deaths needed ways to imagine concepts that had no imaginings.

Some deaths said even Oldest Death had come from that chalice.

Some deaths said that tip of a branch of the tree of life, that arm-like hand grasping the chalice, was attached to a greater tree that reached out its branches into a million, billion universes.

Some said it was all crap that only a young death would believe because no old death had ever talked about actually seeing a tree, a branch, or a chalice. Those deaths, certainly most of the deaths, said the lake was the lake. It was and had always been. If there had ever been anything like the tree of life, the branch, or the chalice, it had long ago been flooded over by the souls of all things. Even if a branch were there, somewhere in the bottom of the lake, it was meaningless to them and their work because it was at the bottom of the lake. Their job was to gather souls, dump the souls, and repeat. What did a tree, a branch, or a cup mean to them and their work?

So, they went on working.

They gathered souls.

They returned the souls to the lake, which returned souls to the rivers, which fed them into streams that took them into Overworld to new bodies, to new growth, to greater wisdom, and to deeper love until at last they were large enough and strong enough and enlightened enough to become the pure, pervasive light of love that shines through all things.

Then, so Ereshkigal had once told her, the pure love souls came back to the lake and stayed there. They touched lesser souls, helping them to grow and change. They mingled with one another and the great heart, the living, breathing universe itself.

"Mingle?" Littlest had asked.

Ereshkigal had sighed an impatient sigh and nodded. "Like your sparks from the ocean deeps. They are part of the life of the ocean, yes?"

"Oh," she said. "Like the web of life thing."

"Yes," Ereshkigal said. "The ocean is alive because they are alive."

"The water isn't alive."

Ereshkigal had stretched her clawed toes, stood, and opened her wings.

Littlest jumped back.

"Afraid, Littlest Death?"

"No," she said, but she hadn't convinced the Sumerian or herself.

"We are connected. My actions affect you. Yours affect me. I am you. You are me."

"I don't get it."

Ereshkigal nodded and flew away.

Now, Littlest Death sat on her worn rock at the edge of the lake. She considered these odd things and the good luck she feared and hoped had finally come her way.

The Threepup napped beside her—heads draped across crossed paws, broad chest rising and falling. Now and then, he jerked or yipped—probably chasing a thrown rock or fighting off some Greek hero trying to wade upstream into Underworld.

She picked up a black pebble and tossed it into the Lake of All Souls.

As it arced outward over the fluid, silver-blue surface, a twinge of guilt touched her. She probably shouldn't toss stones into the souls.

She shook off the silly idea. It wasn't the first time she'd tossed stones into the lake. Souls in the lake didn't feel a stone falling on them any more than individual drops of water in a pond in Overworld could feel it. Like water, they just parted and let the stone sink.

What did she think was going to happen? Wailing? Screaming? Recriminations?

Stupid, she told herself. *The* maybe *chance of one human has made me stupid.*

Still, she wanted the pebble back as she watched it fall into the viscous, glowing lake without sound or splash. Lazy ripples moved outward in fluorescing silver rolls from the place where the stone disappeared.

Absently, alone with her confused hopes, she watched the ripples move outward from the center, coming closer to her on one side and moving away from her on the other.

Eventually, the ripples reached the edge of the lake, and the silver surface lapped gently at the stone near her toes.

The surface calmed.

Just to prove to herself that her concern had been stupid, she tossed another pebble. The ripples expanded, lapped, and calmed again.

Not one scream or lamentation.

She did it again.

And again.

The pebbles entered the Lake of All Souls, and then they were gone. She thought that each soul that came to the lake was gone, too. Just like a pebble, it fell into the lake and was swallowed up by the silver, seamless mass of other souls. Each soul left its flesh in Overworld and ended up here, nothing, gone, meaningless, having never existed at all.

She had brought her bucket full of sparks here thousands upon thousands of times. Each time she dumped the bucket, a million tiny souls poured out. Each time, the sparks melted into the lake. They didn't even make a ripple as large as the stones she tossed. They just disappeared.

It seemed so pointless—so sad.

A rain of pebbles arced out over her head and pelted the surface of the lake.

She jumped up.

The Hydra Hound woke, leapt to his feet, turned, and barked a three-headed Greek chorus.

She followed the Triple Threat's gaze and found Oldest Death, a shade standing in shadows, near the walls of the cavern.

Or, perhaps he was the shadow. He might be all shadows. It was hard to tell.

"Assignment finished?" he asked.

Shame flushed through her. She had meant to go right away. Then, she had meant to go in a little bit. It wasn't like her job was as important as his—or as important as any of the other deaths. Still, Oldest Death hovering over her made her pointedly aware that she had ignored her assignment and settled down next to the lake to worry about things that might not even happen.

And there it was. She hadn't gone because she was afraid it wouldn't happen. She'd go and come back just carrying another bucket of tiny sparks.

She was pretty sure this was not the way to get a promotion.

He floated forward across the cavern floor to her, cocked back a bony hand, and let fly another handful of pebbles. They scattered out over the surface of the lake, pelting the silver sheen and launching a hundred sets of ripples.

"Chaos," she whispered.

Oldest Death laughed.

The hollow sound chilled her.

Then, he asked, "Only one pebble at a time for you?"

She tried to look into his hood, but she found no hope or solace there—only deeper darkness. "I like to watch the ripples coming to the shore."

"Me, too." He moved to stand beside her, and he peered out over the lake. "I sat on that same stone long before any other death had come to be."

Conversation with Oldest Death was not something she had expected. She had expected shaming, shunning, guilt, a lecture. She had expected …

She didn't know what she had expected, but she certainly hadn't expected him to reach down, scratch Left behind his ears, or to sit down on a rock next to her—all of which he did.

"Your turn." He pointed a long, boney finger out at the smooth surface of the lake.

A little terrified, she sat next to him. Slowly, afraid it was a trick, she picked up a pebble and tossed it. As usual, the stone arced outward, fell, and disappeared into the silvery-blue liquid of life.

She glanced sideways at Oldest Death, but he was intent on the point where the stone had disappeared.

There, ripples formed and rolled away from the center point.

Before they reached the shore at her feet, Oldest Death tossed a handful of pebbles into the first few rolling, concentric waves.

The pretty, shimmering, perfectly concentric circles shattered—interrupted by a hundred other center points radiating new ripples.

It upset her. She didn't know why it upset her, but she wanted to tell Oldest Death he was a bit of a turd for messing up her ripples.

She didn't.

After all, that was just not something any death would say to Oldest Death. Certainly, it wasn't the kind of thing Littlest Death could say to any death, and if she had said it to Oldest Death, she'd likely have ended up shuttling amoeba souls for the rest of eternity.

She checked her three-headed shadow to see how he was responding to the rock tossing, but Eternal Rest Rover had already settled back to his nap.

"Every life is a pebble," Oldest Death lectured in nearly the same tones Ereshkigal had used.

"Uh-huh." She suddenly wanted to be at the hospital and reaping the microbes she'd been assigned. Anything would be better than the lecture she now expected.

"So," Oldest Death continued, "Every life creates ripples."

"Well, duh." She couldn't help herself.

He stood and turned away.

Quickly, she said, "I'm sorry. I didn't mean—"

He interrupted her. "One soul."

"One pebble," she said, hoping to convince him she had listened and wasn't really as petulant as she thought she sounded.

"This time, one child. Only one," he said. "Find it. Reap it. Bring it to the lake and rebirth."

She couldn't speak. She wasn't sure she had heard correctly.

But she was sure she had.

By the time she found her voice, Oldest Death had merged into the shadows.

He had come and gone, and she had been too busy being careful of him to ask the questions that were important.

Okay. He had made his assignment for her clear. She didn't just have vague permission to retrieve a human soul. She had been assigned a human soul.

This was it!

He believed she could do it. She had to believe, too.

Littlest Death stood up, took up her bucket, and strode toward the river to 21st Century America and her duty.

Dead Head Dog sprang up and capered along behind her, grabbing at her billowing robes and totally messing up her determined dignity.

Going to Overworld

One soul …

Gather a bucket full of sparks and one human soul.

While she ran, she said it to herself over and over.

21st Century America. It was a world of ignorance, illusions, confusions, desperation, prejudices, and understanding. She would have to be careful. It wasn't like the old days when only a few major rivers flowed out from the lake to entire continents. Thousands, if not millions, of belief systems competed and intermingled where she was going.

The feeder streams into her destination in time and space began at the lake as a river, but the river split and split again, and again. The rivers became streams. The streams became rivulets. The rivulets became trickles, and the trickles led to families, organizations, regions, tribes, and weird, distributed social groups made up of members spread across the planet and connected only by the thinnest electronic threads. Each grouping of humans embraced their own beliefs—their own metaphors for life and death.

Littlest Death hoped the soul she'd been sent for wasn't an atheist. She'd heard about atheists. They were the hardest. Navigating back to the underworld in the soul's expected total absence of experience was tricky at best. Once, she'd heard one of the angels, Azrael, say it was like hauling a bag of rocks through fog at moonless midnight on the bottom of the sea.

Littlest Death wasn't sure what that all meant, but she had been to the bottom of the sea. It wasn't fun.

Of course, Azrael wasn't always reliable. He was a meta for three of the most destructive religions on Earth, so he was tired and cranky most of the time. She just couldn't completely trust a Christian/Jewish/Islamic angel of death about atheist souls, but she was sure she didn't want to find out about atheists on her first trip out.

No.

Her first human soul wouldn't be an atheist. She didn't think Oldest Death would send her for a really hard retrieval on her first run.

Then a thought occurred to her.

He might.

She slowed her hurried trot along the banks of the river of souls.

He just might send her after an atheist if he thought it would be so hard she would fail. He might think it was a way to make her more content harvesting the little sparks of life she had been gathering for a thousand years.

The Pushy Puppy nipped at her robes.

She swished them aside. She had to think about this.

All three puppy heads grasped her robes and pulled her downstream.

She stumbled forward. "Stop that!"

Left released, looked up at her, and whined. Center and Right still pulled at her.

"Bad dog!"

Whining Left joined the others tugging on her robes.

She stumbled forward again, and not far ahead she saw a split in the river of souls. Not far beyond that, she saw another.

The dog was right. She should get on with it. If Oldest Death wanted her to fail, she would know soon enough. If she were late for her pickup, she would most certainly fail, and that wouldn't be Oldest Death's fault. That would be all hers, and she'd be a worse laughing stock than she already was.

Okay, then. She'd show them what she could do. She'd bring back a bucket full of a million sparks, and she'd have a human by the hand.

She gathered up her robes and strode downstream.

The Trihound released her and trotted along beside.

She navigated each branching with the unerring knowing natural to all deaths who have been given their assignment. The Beast with Three Heads followed, yipping and dancing around her feet as if she were a living girl and he was her new puppy on some springtime outing.

The river split. The stream split. The creek split. The rivulet split. Finally, she stood at a fork looking down at that pale, shining trickle of souls flowing into the world of American medicine and beliefs.

Close up, the many, hair-like strands splitting out from what she had thought was the last trickle became visible. It stunned her that such a tiny flow could split again and again and again.

There had to be a thousand, thousand tiny, tiny fingers of soul reaching outward into Overworld. She had no idea which one went to her hospital.

"So much for the unerring knowing natural to all deaths," she said.

The Pester Puppy sat, scratched itself, and watched. Two heads cocked to the left and one to the right. All six ears stood more-or-less erect. Well, they tried, but only one ear succeeded. The others all flopped off to the side an inch or so above a fuzzy, black hell-hound skull. All six glowing red eyes stared at her.

"What are you staring at?" she asked.

Left shook as if it had taken a chill or chosen to answer her with, "Nothing. I'm just sitting here."

She tried to feel her way forward, but the tug—the vague feeling that she needed to set foot just there, just to the right or to the left or along that tiny flow of silvery soul stuff was too confusing. It was still strong, but it could have guided her in any of ten directions. She might come out into the Overworld in Denver or San Francisco for all the difference she felt between one trickle and the next.

Center barked impatiently.

"Help or be quiet," she said.

The single tail thumped against black stone. As if the Black Beagle of Hades had understood her, all three heads dipped to rivulets and started sniffing.

"Don't be ridiculous," she said. "If I can't find it, you can't find it."

Left and Right lifted from their search, stiffened, and pointed along one of the middle rivulets. Center looked up at her and yipped in agreement.

"I can't screw this up," she said.

All three heads barked their creepy, baying chorus.

She started forward.

So did they.

She stopped. "You are not a death," she said.

Hell Hunter sat and whimpered.

"You are not coming."

Center barked plaintively.

"No," she said firmly.

Underworldpup sat.

Fairly sure the dog would stay, she felt carefully for the way forward. She chose her next step, and she was through the veil and into Overworld.

The Hospital

Brilliant fluorescent white light surrounded her, and the smells of liberally applied antiseptics hiding the offal and bile smells of human misery assaulted her. She knew that smell. She'd been to hospitals before to gather up the sparks from petri dishes, toilets, autoclaves, sink traps, toilet pipes, ventilation shafts, and tile floors.

Imagining the hospital to be a good sign since Oldest Death had specifically mentioned it, she felt for her tug, for that feeling that she was where she should be and on the path to the dead or dying she had been sent for.

Ahead and to her right.

Unseen by the bustling, hustling hospital staff and the sad, anxious people waiting in chairs or pacing in corridors and waiting areas, she moved along hallways under the buzzing fluorescents.

Left.

She turned and passed through double doors into a children's ward.

Okay, she thought. So far, so good.

By the lake, Oldest Death had said she'd be picking up a child, but she had been too worried and excited at the time to think about that. Now, she had no choice. She told herself that a child should be easy—very easy.

Most children believed something about life and afterlife. Sometimes, they believed some very strange things—at least until they learned to conform to the stranger things adults told them to believe. Once, she had overheard a death talking about a child who believed that the afterlife was a bowl of chocolate pudding he would live in forever and ever.

The death had said the slog through pudding to the lake had been rough.

Littlest Death figured she'd take chocolate pudding over Azrael's description of atheism.

Regardless, once she met the soul she'd know what it believed. She said, "That has to be how it works, right?"

She turned to look for the three bobbing, drooling heads of the Canine of Confirmation. Of course, they were gone—left behind in Underworld.

Maybe Treble Trouble Pups couldn't pass through the veil. She supposed that made more sense than the idea that all three heads had learned obedience.

Oldest Death *had* said the soul was a child's. She was sure he had.

Now that she was here, she didn't want to bring back a doctor or nurse—or a parent.

Adults did die in children's wings. Sometimes, they had strokes. Sometimes, they had heart attacks. She knew what this place was about. It was about money and death.

Another death passed through a door ahead of her. Tall, white-robed, winged, and glowing, Azrael paused when he saw her. Beside him, hiding behind his bright thread-bare robes, a little girl of maybe three clutched an ethereal stuffed dog to her chest with one hand and held Azrael's hand with her other.

Littlest Death saw no reason to be rude. More to the girl than Azrael, she said, "Hello."

The girl slipped farther behind the robes of her death.

Azrael, tired and worn looking like always, peered down at Littlest and said, "Autoclaves are near the operating rooms two floors down."

Littlest Death knew she should just go about her business. Word that she had retrieved a human soul would get out soon enough. She didn't need to flaunt her new status, but a thousand years of deaths looking down on her was too much. Of all the metas, an angel that served Christian, Islamic, and Judaic beliefs should understand respect. She wanted him to show her just a little respect. Didn't she deserve a little respect? She had worked hard. She had taken every little spark she'd been assigned back to the Lake of All Souls. She had carried billions and billions of fungi, bugs, and germs without complaining—much.

Hell, she had probably carried billions more souls than this entitled, confused angel had, and this time she was bringing back a human child just like him.

She might not gain his admiration, but he had no right to look down on her.

She drew herself up as tall as she could—almost up to his chest. "I'm here for a human," she said.

The laugh of an angel is terrifying.

The little girl peeked out at Littlest Death. She looked scared. Tears welled up in her dark, doe eyes.

Littlest Death wondered for a moment if a departing soul could feel fear or sadness. She supposed they could. After all, their life metaphors still influenced their after death journey to the lake. Littlest Death imagined they might feel pain, sadness, or joy—maybe for a while, anyway. Of course, she couldn't be sure of that. She'd never had to think about it before. She'd never carried a human soul, and she knew fungi and paramecium felt nothing once they passed over.

At least, she thought they felt nothing. It had never come up. They certainly didn't cry.

Glistening, silver soul tears rolled down the girl's dark cheeks. They looked just like a tiny trickle of spirit flowing over the basalt in Underworld.

Littlest felt a strange and sudden urge to say something to the girl, but she had no idea what to say.

Azrael shook his haloed head and dragged the child along behind him, through the veil, and into the silvery light on the banks of the rivers of Underworld.

Littlest Death caught a brief glimpse of the Pointless Pooch still sitting and waiting for her. Then, the veil closed, the little girl disappeared, and Azrael was gone—probably already spreading rumors about her foolish pride.

The Child

Three people held vigil outside the room. The pacing woman clutching a rosary looked like she might be visited by a death soon—probably Azrael. Her tight, pale features were drawn downward. As if pulled by invisible weights, her shoulders bent forward and down, which made her back look bowed. No makeup could hide the sharpness of her cheekbones, the dark circles under her eyes, or their redness.

Those eyes had been cried dry.

Littlest Death had never seen it before, but Ereshkigal had once told her about it—a human face drained by grief even before a death had brought release for someone they loved.

Ereshkigal had told her that only a death could bring relief and healing to a person like that.

The woman probably grieved for the child inside the room. If Ereshkigal was right, the healing could only start once Littlest Death helped that soul return to the lake.

Humans were certainly more complicated than paramecia.

This trip wasn't going to be a dip-and-dash affair. She sort of wished it were. Some of her happiest memories came from days when she competed with herself to see how many sparks she could get with her bucket in a single dip and how fast she could return to the lake in a mad dash.

Apparently, humans required time and care.

She imagined that the first trick she had to learn was to ignore the people outside the room. Only one thing mattered—the soul she'd been assigned.

Still, she couldn't help looking at the others. Every detail of every inch of the hallway and the people in it seemed more important than any edge of glowing muck in an alpine lake or any high water mark in a sewer line had ever seemed.

The middle-aged man who leaned forward in his chair, tired eyes following the pacing woman, seemed ready to leap forward and catch her if she fainted. His narrow, unshaven face was hard, as if he had long ago given up on grieving and moved on to rage. Anger seemed the only thing animating him, and Littlest wondered about what humans thought happened after flesh. What gave them so much pain and anger?

She was pretty sure they all died.

As far as she knew, none of them had ever avoided meeting a death. Every single soul left the flesh, went back to the lake, down the rivers, into the rivulets, and finally into a new body.

She had heard legends of transcendent souls—souls that had become love in the lake for a time and eventually, one last time, went to flesh to teach. The stories said those souls moved beyond even the brightness of love that let them mingle in the Lake of All Souls. If a soul had been in flesh enough times, had lived as brightness and love in the lake, and had returned to flesh to teach and learn whatever final knowing souls were supposed to learn, they returned to the very center of the Lake of All Souls. There, something happened to them.

She'd heard about it, but she had always heard about it second hand. A death knew a death who knew a death who saw a soul enter the lake, glow more brightly than the other souls, move toward the center of the lake, and then be lifted up into the chalice held high by the tree of life. There, the soul spread outward and became. . .

She usually stopped listening about there. The ending was always different and always weird. It was a lot to take in, and she got bored with the stories because they were never about how she could get promoted. They weren't about planaria. They weren't about where she could get a bigger bucket and how she could gather in more souls in order to be recognized for her work.

Those stories were always about humans that nobody had ever really seen or met.

Littlest Death figured the stories were just more tales the deaths told to tease her.

A thousand years, billions of sparks gathered, and they still teased her because she was the newbie.

Today, that would change.

She refocused on the humans. Humans die. They all die. Watching these people, she couldn't help wondering why they seemed so attached to someone else's flesh. They seemed to be in so much pain over one soul about to be freed—and it wasn't even their soul. Their bodies felt no pain. Their flesh went on.

The third person outside the room was a child—probably a brother. His thumbs tapped at the glowy side of the facephone thing he peered into. He was maybe ten or twelve. She wasn't sure. He was about Littlest's size, and he just looked tired. Littlest Death imagined that the boy was taking it better than the parents because he might be young enough to remember the love of the Lake of All Souls.

Littlest knew from eavesdropping on arguing deaths that when a child's time came they were generally more comfortable with heading back to the lake.

Azrael had said it was because they were innocent and "closer to God, Allah, Yahweh."

Ammit had said it was because their souls were lighter than an ostrich feather.

Ereshkigal had said it was because they were closer to their last time in the lake and didn't fear what came next.

Littlest Death realized she had been hovering around the family speculating on the plight of humans because she was nervous about taking her first human soul.

She gathered her resolve and slid through the closed door into the room.

Two beds. Bright lights. Two children. Both were very young—too young for full-sized beds. At the foot of the beds along one white wall, a table holding a scattering of brightly colored blocks, toy cars, puzzles, and coloring books showed signs that someone had been playing there.

A plastic car had fallen to the floor and been kicked against the wall under the table. A deck of black cards covered in pictures seemed to be arranged carefully in a pattern.

Littlest Death naturally focused on the color of the table of toys.

Toys.

She remembered that human children did things that had no meaning, and that was supposed to be good. They played like the Dog of Distraction. The little girl she had seen on the way here had even loved her toy so much that she had managed to carry an ethereal form of it into Underworld.

Human children loved toys.

She glanced at the beds. Both children slept. Two identical machines stood between the two beds. Quiet, regular beeps came from both machines. Quiet, regular breaths came from both children. Really, the only difference between them was the shape of their faces and the fact that one had hair and the other did not.

The black-haired child had a nearly crimson face shaped like a moon. He was nearer the door. The bald girl had a white, narrow face and deep-shadowed eye sockets.

Neither their faces nor their breathing and machines gave Littlest a clue as to which might be ready for her help.

One of them certainly was. She knew that from the look of the family members outside.

A thing on the table of toys chirped like a bird. It was a sound of surprise and release—an almost pleasant sound of sudden, unexpected peace. It reminded her of a bush wren she had almost retrieved after a sharp-shinned hawk had hit it hard from above.

Excited, she'd been about to scoop up the wren's soul when St. Francis had shown up to take it. His look of kindness was worse than the glares of contempt she got from other deaths. Retrospectively, she thought maybe he was okay. He'd been a peaceful, kind death gathering animal souls long before Christians had believed him into his monk robes. She guessed becoming a meta hadn't really changed him much.

Littlest Death went to the table. Among the blocks, the cars, the crayons, and the half-colored pages, she found a flat plastic electrical toy device. She had heard of them—laptablets or something.

One of the children had been playing a game on it.

Littlest Death tapped at the screen. It flickered. Candies shattered and moved, but she quickly discovered that the laptablet thing needed flesh-covered fingers to work well. Still, she stared at the brightly colored candies on the screen and wondered once again what play like this was for—why crushing candies was important to humans. For answers, she searched the other items on the table.

Her gaze wandered to the black cards in rows and stacks. This was clearly a more physical game than the one on the tablet. It wasn't all fleshy tapping, bright lights, and the surprised sound of wrens. The cards had pictures and numbers and meaning. The card game was a thinking and imagining game.

She set her bucket on the floor and tried to puzzle out the meaning of the cards. Caverns, dragons, wheels, towers, monsters.

It made no sense to her, but she wasn't flesh and blood like a child.

Behind her, one of the children said, "I'm almost out."

Littlest Death turned. The dark-haired, round-faced child had lifted his head and was looking directly at her.

"You can see me?" Littlest Death asked.

The child's dark curls bounced when he nodded.

Well, that answered the question as to which soul she was to take away.

"The cards," he said. "It's Dungeon Solitaire."

"I knew that," Littlest lied.

"I'm almost out. A perfect game." The child smiled knowingly, as if he knew Littlest Death had lied.

"Good," she tried to cover.

He went on. "You pull the cards and lay them out. Some give you skills. Some mess you up. Some are monsters. Some treasures. You keep laying them out to go deeper."

Littlest turned back and looked over the cards. She began to see a pattern. She said, "If bad things happen, you use your skills."

"Uh-huh."

She pointed to a card. "What's this one?"

"Ace of Cups. Not real good, but I had torches."

Littlest said, "The picture looks like something from a story I heard."

The child breathed heavily, recovering from talking.

Littlest Death checked on the bald child. Nothing had changed. She slept. The machines both beeped steadily. The little chest rose and fell.

"This is playing?" she asked.

Curls bobbed. "Uh-huh."

"Can you show me how?"

"I'm kinda sick," he said.

"Play helps if you're sick?"

"I played some yesterday. I got really tired."

Littlest Death thought about how hard it was for the child to talk. He couldn't teach her to play. It occurred to her that she had to take the soul anyway, and now was as good as later.

Of course, once she took it, she'd have to immediately return to Underworld. That was how it worked.

But she could stop Overworld time. She picked up her bucket and tapped the rim. The machines stopped beeping. The bald girl stopped breathing. The dark-haired boy froze in mid gasp for breath.

Littlest crossed the room and took the child's hand.

A brilliant, silver-blue light surrounded the child, and the body eternal rose from the flesh.

The child was brighter than any soul she had ever seen. She was a death, so she had stood next to the Lake of All Souls in the light of a billion, trillion souls, and she still had to squint a bit to look at this child's soul.

Of course, her experience with newly taken human souls was limited. She only saw their souls when other deaths were bringing them to the lake. She figured this soul was really fresh, so it was especially bright. After all, humans were different than the sparks she usually carried.

The child smiled and nodded to her. He said, "Oh. I understand now."

"What?" Littlest Death asked.

"Well, everything," he said.

Littlest Death didn't know what to make of that, so she said, "Can you show me how to play?"

"Of course," he said, and he did.

Together, they played the card game through four full games until Littlest Death understood it and could play it by herself.

A feeling of … *of* … *what*? What was the feeling that came into her when she managed to get her meager treasure out of the dungeon? "I feel something," she said.

"Pleasure," the fresh soul offered.

"Sort of."

"Accomplishment. You solved the puzzle."

"Is that what fun is? Feeling good about solving a puzzle?"

The glowing child soul wrinkled its nose and shook his glowing, curly head slightly. "Aren't we supposed to go somewhere?"

Littlest Death had forgotten about abusing her time-stopping power. Startled by the soul's clarity and directness, she nodded. "Yes. I suppose so." She took a last longing look at the cards and started time again.

Immediately, one of the machines made a loud, urgent buzz.

A moment later, a doctor and several nurses stormed into the room.

The curly-haired, red-faced little boy's chest had ceased to rise and fall.

His ethereal hand found hers, and she tugged him toward the door.

"I'll help you go on," she said.

"And I'll help you," he said, as if this kind of thing happened to him every day.

It seemed an odd thing for a child's soul to say even if children dealt with death better than adults, but the chaos in the room flustered her. It was, after all, her first time, and the child was probably a bit shocked, too.

She remembered the fearful, tearful face of the little girl hiding behind Azrael's robes.

Gathering the buckets of tiny sparks had never required her to speak to souls. She was sure some of the more experienced deaths had worked out what to say to sooth a newly returned soul, but she'd never thought to ask them about it.

She wanted to do everything right. Even though the boy seemed calm, she wanted to say something.

Littlest Death tried to imagine what Ereshkigal would have said.

"Thank you," she said. There. That was good to say. "Everything is Okay." That was good to say, too.

She pulled the child's hand, and they moved out through the door just as it opened and the family came in.

"It will be," the little soul said. "Eventually."

To the Lake

The boy didn't make a sound the whole way back to Underworld, but the Puppy of Demonic Destruction waited for them just inside the veil.

Meeting the dancing, weaving, leaping Triple Threat, the boy smiled, glowed a little brighter, and said, "Is this your dog?"

Littlest Death waved at the puppy, "Get away from him."

The Doom Dog hadn't ever listened before, and he didn't now.

Cadaver Canine sniffed the boy with one head, licked his face with another, and tugged playfully on his glowing hospital gown with the third. The hellish tail did chopping circles in the air.

Littlest Death said, "You are an embarrassment to Underworld."

"There wasn't a dog to greet me last time I was here," the boy said. "I like this."

Littlest Death knew a few things, so she corrected him. "You can't remember your other deaths until you join the lake."

The boy laughed and petted Center on the flat top of his head. "I can," he said. "And there were no dogs."

Littlest Death pulled hard on his hand to separate the fresh soul from the enthusiastic attentions of three hound heads. She said, "Who is the expert here?"

The boy followed, saying, "My last father used to say an expert is a person whose mouth is open so often that they can't hear."

Annoyed, Littlest Death said, "Humans can't remember the last time they died. Every death knows souls can only remember other lives and deaths in the lake. It's part of why it's a lake—so you can mingle with other souls, share memories, learn, and eventually choose a new path and follow the river that will take you where you need to go next."

The soul followed her silently upstream for a bit. The Dark Denizen padded along behind. After a while, the boy said, "I think everyone who dies should be met by a puppy."

Trying to be kind, she said, "Maybe, but certainly not this one."

Hound at their heels, they continued upstream. The child, who was clearly not nearly as frightened, surprised, or confused as Azrael's little girl had been, looked all around him—taking in the dark caverns, the silver glow of the ever-widening river of souls, and the happy cavorting of Puppy Horror Hound.

As the shores of the Lake of All Souls came into view, the child soul said, "Last time, I was a Christian."

"Please," Littlest Death said. "We're almost there. Soon, you won't have to make things up to make yourself feel better."

"An angel met me," the soul said. "Azrael," he added. "He was really tired and sad."

Littlest stumbled on her robes. The soul shouldn't have known Azrael by name.

Then, it occurred to her that the beliefs that gave Azrael form might have been part of the soul's life on Earth. Since three belief systems made him a meta, a whole lot of humans must know the name.

She steadied herself, watched her footing, and pulled the soul along the shortest possible path to the lake. She said, "We deaths only look like angels for Christians."

"I know," the soul said. "I remember, and my uncle, Lawrence, was there, too."

Littlest Death stopped, turned, and looked down at the soul. "What?"

Now, the boy tugged on Littlest Death, pulling her closer to the lake. "When I followed that poor angel Azrael to the lake, Uncle Lawrence was near the shore waiting for me."

She didn't think the boy could have made that up. Certainly, his experiences in life wouldn't have included a family member in the lake separating itself out to welcome him in.

She shook off her unease. Guesses and children's stories didn't matter. Whoever he was supposed to meet and mingle with would be there. They might rise up to meet him. They might not. Either way, she doubted it would be Uncle Lawrence from some other life.

She followed the boy, and as they got closer, excitement started to take hold. She was about to deliver her first ever human soul to the Lake of All Souls. Soon, she would be a true death instead of just a death for sparks from worms and germs. She'd be the bringer of millions per bucket and humans whenever she wanted. Nobody would laugh at her then.

In another thousand years, she'd be using her bucket to scoop up humans by the millions. She'd be the best death ever. The other deaths would come to her for advice, and she wouldn't be mean like them. She would smile and nod and help them solve any problems they had. She'd always be kind to the lesser deaths.

At the shore, The Ditsy Death Dog danced around them.

The boy faced her, grew brighter still, smiled broadly, and said, "I'm sorry."

"Excuse me?" She instantly regretted saying it. Humans probably said all kinds of pointless things before they stepped into the lake and melted and mingled. She decided to treat it as if he had thanked her. Pretending she hadn't said anything, she nodded in what she hoped was a stoic and dignified fashion. She said, "You're welcome."

The foolish frolicking of the whelp at their feet ruined her attempted gravitas.

"Oh, just go," she said.

The soul let go of her hand and turned to face the lake.

"Go on," she said. "There's nothing to be afraid of."

"Yes," he said. "Try not to worry too much about what you've done."

Child-spoken nonsense born of fear. That was okay. It was almost over.

Except for the odd things the soul said, coming back to Underworld had been like coming back alone. They hadn't shifted into one of the belief metaphors souls liked to drag along with them after leaving flesh. She told herself that was why Oldest Death assigned her a child. In flesh, the boy was young and hadn't completely embraced whatever beliefs surrounded him.

That the soul spoke nonsense before it entered the lake didn't mean anything. Leaving the flesh was disorienting.

Yes. It all made sense, she told herself.

The boy stepped away from the shore.

She expected him to linger a moment on the surface then sink into the silver mingling of all souls the same way the tiny sparks did—only bigger.

He didn't.

She had not expected him to walk out onto the surface of the lake.

He did.

The Damned Dog stopped jumping and chasing its tail. All three heads stilled. It plopped down on its butt beside her. Left pressed against her robe and thigh. All six ears perked straight up.

The brilliant, silver soul in a split-backed hospital gown strode casually toward the center of the lake.

There, in the glowing silver-blue surface, a greater brightness appeared—and grew.

As if she had tossed a pebble into the lake at the feet of the soul, ripples rose and flowed outward. From the center of the concentric waves, a blinding white light shone. At its center, a chalice that might have been made of the heart of a sun rose. As it lifted upward, living souls poured from it and into the surrounding lake.

Beneath the sun-gold chalice, a supporting palm and the finger-like branches of an ancient tree appeared and rose upward until a gnarled, wooden wrist gave way to an arm, the arm to an elbow, and the elbow to an oaken upper arm.

The child soul, now almost too bright to look at, shot a brilliant, blissful grin over his shoulder. Then, he reached forward, took the chalice, sipped from it, and placed it back in the hand of the tree of life.

As the branch and chalice sank back into the lake, the soul's boy-like form burned brighter still even while it became nearly transparent.

To Littlest Death, it seemed that the brilliance that was the boy grew taller, wider, broader. He became an expanding bubble of light that was no longer a child but somehow still the boy she had brought to Underworld.

She lifted the loose sleeve of her robe to shield her eyes from the brightness that had once been shaped like a child.

The dog lay down on his belly. Eyes closed tight, he tried to cover all his faces with his paws.

Then, the soul was gone.

Just gone.

Littlest Death blinked and searched the cavernous expanse of the lake at the heart of Underworld.

The surface still glowed, but it now seemed dull and dark to her.

She had seen him standing on the surface of the lake, glowing. She had seen the glow expand until his form was gone. She had hidden her eyes. When she could see again, he was just gone as if he had never been in Underworld at all.

"Uh-oh," she whispered.

She was pretty sure what had just happened wasn't supposed to happen.

She thought through the events of her day. She was pretty sure she'd done something wrong, but she didn't know what. She did know that Oldest Death would not be happy about it.

Hades Puppy lifted its heads and peered at her—all six ears at half-flop and all six burning red eyes focused and worried.

"I know," she said. "Not good."

Together, they searched the surface of the Lake of All Souls again.

No sign of the soul, the branch, or the chalice remained.

The only signs that anything had happened at all were the gentle slap of ripples against the shore at her feet.

After a moment, not even the ripples remained.

"Not good at all," she said.

What Happened?

Okay, she told herself. *Gone. The soul probably joined the lake while my eyes were covered.*

Or the myths are true.

No.

Maybe.

Either way, it was good. Right? Even better if nobody had seen whatever had just happened.

She glanced along the dark shore in both directions. The liquid souls filling the lake glowed their normal silver-blue light. Normal black shadows among rocks and craggy walls hid any living or unliving things.

She checked the Dog of Darkness to see if he showed any sign of having sensed anyone or anything nearby.

Left and Right rested on crossed paws, drooling and eyes half closed. Apparently, the whole experience had been so exhausting that a nap was upon them.

Only Center watched her—burning red eyes and quivering black nose all focused on her. Certainly, he would scent any wandering deaths or errant souls.

Okay. I delivered the soul, she told herself.

Yeah. But it didn't melt into the lake.

Might have.

Don't lie to yourself. You know it didn't.

Still, she argued with herself, *good.*

It must be good. If the stories she'd heard were true, the chalice and tree of life only appeared when a soul moved on from the cycle of Overworld and Underworld.

It hit her.

By all the gods and goddesses invented by man, she had seen it. As far as she knew, she was the only one who had ever actually seen it.

No. That couldn't be right. Oldest Death had to have seen it before. For that matter, he had to have known this soul was transcendent before he gave her the assignment.

It was an honor. That was it.

Oh, how she wanted that to be true. Certainly, she'd been excited to take her first human soul, but she had a little trouble believing that Oldest Death intended for her to take a transcendent soul.

No. He'd have taken care of such a soul himself.

She looked down at Hades Puppy and said, "Wouldn't he?"

Center cocked his blocky head. Left opened his sleepy eyes and shook himself.

Rear foot to Left's left ear, Carrion Canine scratched. Left's head bowed low, eyes closed in ecstasy.

Center turned a jealous gaze on blissful Left.

Littlest Death thought maybe Center didn't get much scratching—being in the middle and farthest from both hind legs.

The scratch-shake woke up Right, but he looked her dead in the eyes and cocked his head a little, as if to say, you are in such deep dog doo now.

"Maybe he meant me to do it," she said to Monster Mutt. "Maybe it was a reward for a thousand years of service doing small souls."

Right shook his head violently, as if trying to shake flea ghosts from his fur.

Even if Oldest Death had meant her to retrieve a transcendent soul, she decided she should tell someone what had happened. If Oldest Death had rewarded her, she'd celebrate. If he had made a mistake, she'd get points for telling him.

Of course, she might need help telling him. She didn't think she wanted to tell him alone.

No. Not alone.

She'd find one of the deaths that hadn't been quite so mean to her over the millennia. Her first choice was Ereshkigal. She was older than most. She'd seen and done more than most, and she almost never made fun of Littlest Death.

Sure. That was the thing to do—talk to Ereshkigal. She'd help.

Checking with Other Deaths

On the way to find her not-quite friend, Littlest Death realized she hadn't really considered all the possibilities.

The Big Black Dog of Death bounced around her, excited for walkies, and Littlest Death thought, maybe, just maybe, Oldest Death hadn't made a mistake or intended her to bring back a transcendent soul.

Maybe, I made the mistake.

That changed things.

Ereshkigal was not the death to talk to if the mistake hadn't been Oldest Death's. Ereshkigal was good if Oldest Death had known. She'd offer advice on how to be humble. She'd know how to tell the story so he saved face.

But if Littlest Death screwed up, she might need to know how to soften the story. Ereshkigal …

Well, she couldn't bear to see the disappointment on her almost-friend's face if she made a mistake of such profound magnitude that the only transcended soul in forever had transcended without … without … without whatever was supposed to be there or happen when a transcending soul went wherever transcended souls went.

"Oh, this is bad," she said.

The Barking Banshee chuffed three-toned agreement.

Littlest needed an old death—probably a meta. She needed to talk to a death who embodied sneaky and sly.

Baast.

Baast would be better for finding out what really happened.

Baast was clever, too. She'd be better for fixing things if Littlest Death had created a problem and didn't want to tell anyone. Baast knew secrets and rituals and magics. Baast was really old. Maybe Baast liked to torment Littlest Death, but at least they talked. Baast didn't like Littlest Death as much as Ereshkigal. Baast was a cat. She didn't really like anybody.

So, that was good.

Littlest didn't search long before she found Baast sitting on a stone dais overlooking a shoal of papyrus reeds in the glowing, flowing Underworld Nile. The goddess stared off over the flow. Her cat eyes looked almost hypnotized by the glowing whirls, swirls, and ripples.

Suddenly, Littlest Death didn't really want to bother the Egyptian.

That Baast's ancient stretch of the river had such fine, Egyptian details meant that people had been believing the same thing, or close enough, for so long that the beliefs had imposed themselves almost permanently on the metaphor of afterlife.

Baast, Isis, Anubis, and Ammit were powerful metas. They had been deaths a long time, and they had been metas for more than six thousand years. Baast was oldest and most powerful among them, and Littlest Death hoped that meant she had seen more, done more, and made more mistakes. A death that had made a lot of mistakes might know a lot about fixing them.

Beyond the dais, here and there, the silver-blue surface stirred as if an individual soul were impatient to step up and out of the flow and into its new, waiting flesh.

The Cur of Corpses danced and circled at her feet, pretending his excitement had nothing to do with the cat goddess.

Littlest Death did her best to stride confidently in spite of Doom Dog's dance. If all was well, she didn't want to appear to be guilty before she knew. If all was not as it should be, she didn't want to telegraph the fact before she knew.

In fact, if all was not well, she was starting to realize that she didn't want any death to know about it—not one.

Every step closer to the hypnotized Baast made Littlest Death more certain she had screwed up, but she didn't know exactly how.

She willed her stride to stay steady. Another step.

Knowing how was important. Baast might be able to help. It would all be fine. After all, it was her first human soul. There had to be other deaths who had messed up their first human assignments. Every death had to have a first time, didn't they? There just had to have been others like her. In millions of years of thousands and thousands of deaths gathering in souls, she couldn't be the first to screw up.

She froze and silently begged the breathing universe to let there have been others.

Baast watched the silvery surface.

A timeless, Underworld moment passed. It might have been years. It might have been seconds.

The Hound of Humiliation settled into tugging at Littlest's robes.

Baast's feline voice broke the trance of timelessness. "Not as exciting as you thought?"

Littlest Death didn't understand. She checked the river's surface to see if Baast saw something she hadn't.

Baast added, "Your first human soul."

"Oh," Littlest said, hoping for another moment to gather her wits and decide where to start.

Baast said, "Still think millions are more than one, or was it much the same as a paramecium?"

"Uh," Littlest managed.

Center nipped at her ankle. Left yipped.

Littlest swiped at Center. "Yeah," she said. "Pretty much."

"I was disappointed, too." Baast turned her head to face Littlest Death. Chilling yellow cat eyes glowed inside her raised hood.

Littlest tried to imagine what her own face looked like peering out from hooded shadows. She doubted it chilled other deaths or human souls. It certainly hadn't chilled the soul she'd lost.

And she was suddenly completely sure she had lost it.

Whatever she had done wasn't what Baast was talking about, but she needed to know more. "Well," she said. "I was a little surprised."

"Oh?" Pressing into her crossed legs, Baast stood and rotated like a cat-faced screw until her legs uncrossed and her whole body faced Littlest. From the dais, Baast towered over Littlest.

One glowing cat eye narrowed in question.

Dark Dog jumped back. All three heads growled.

"Well," Littlest said. "You know, right?"

Baast wasn't put off by the vague comment. "Know what, Littlest One?"

"You know. Like, the whole grieving family and disappearing in the Lake of All Souls thing."

"Ah," Baast said. "Yes. Humans do grieve. That's part of what makes them so special."

"And the disappearing thing," she repeated.

"Really?" Baast said. "That surprised you?"

Littlest Death shuffled her feet and kicked a pebble. "Well, I guess," she mumbled.

Baast laughed. "A little glow. A little flow. The soul is off downstream to a new life."

"Uh-huh," Littlest said. "New life."

Baast said, "I would have expected it to be about the same as dumping a spark into the lake."

Puppy of Sorrows yipped in agreement.

"Uh-huh." Littlest turned in her cowl a little to hide her face, and she crossed her arms to hug herself tight.

Baast said, "Always the same. Never changes."

"Never?"

"You've dumped millions of your buckets, have you ever seen anything different?"

"No," she said.

"Think you'll take on more?"

"Buckets?"

"Humans."

"Somebody," Littlest said, "must bring in the bucket loads."

A little red flicker appeared in the cat goddess's eyes. "Oldest will decide."

"Yeah." Littlest thought she saw a flash of fang revealed by a smile. Then, it was gone.

Baast asked, "Have you reported to Oldest?"

"Just got back," Littlest said.

The goddess pulled back her hood. She regarded Littlest Death for a moment and seemed to come to some solemn decision.

Quick as any great hunting cat, Baast launched herself toward Littlest.

Too late, Littlest tried to jump back.

The elder goddess landed beside her and gently placed a dark-furred, long-fingered hand on her shoulder. "Thank you," Baast said in a solemn voice Littlest had never heard from her before.

The Beagle of Betrayal wagged its tail.

Littlest scuffed her feet a little, pretending she hadn't tried to escape. Finally, she said, "Um, for what?"

"You brought your first soul celebration to me. I am honored." The ancient Egyptian goddess bowed deeply.

Littlest detected no sarcasm or condescension. The bow and thanks felt uncharacteristically sincere.

Baast stood straight.

Littlest Death stammered and looked away from the cat's eyes. "Well …" she shrugged.

Baast's hand fell away.

"I mean," Littlest went on. "Well, you've always been less mean than some of the others."

Baast turned away and started downstream toward Overworld. Over her shoulder, she said, "I expected you to go to Ereshkigal."

"Soon."

Baast chuckled.

Littlest didn't like that chuckle. It had too much cat in it and not enough kind.

Still walking away, Baast said, "Good luck with Oldest, Littlest Death."

"What? Why?"

"You'll understand soon."

"Understand what?" Littlest tried to follow, but the Dog of Deflection held her back by the robes.

Baast didn't break stride. As she disappeared around a bend, Littlest heard her last words. "Oldest Death is waiting."

Standing alone trying to pull her robes free by the Underworld Nile, Littlest wasn't sure what to do. She was sure that other deaths didn't get assigned to transcendent souls. Certainly not on their first time.

At least, Baast hadn't. She'd have bragged about it.

She yanked hard and the Demon of Doggishness released her.

Maybe Littlest should talk to another death. Maab, maybe, or one of the Valkyries. They didn't like her, but they didn't get as much work as they had once. They were certainly talkative among themselves. If she got them talking about it to one another, she might learn something new. Maybe there were things older deaths didn't tell younger deaths until after their first human soul.

And the Valkyries weren't Ereshkigal.

And that thought told her she was hiding. In her core, she knew there was just no possible way what she had just done was intended by Oldest Death.

She had screwed up, and she was going to have to tell him.

"Poop," she said to the Pooch of Perdition. "Just, poop."

Three gleeful yips of agreement came back.

Reporting to Oldest Death

Nobody, living or dead, had ever wanted Oldest Death's undivided attention, but Littlest most certainly had it now. All the darkness that made up the absence of life inside his robes seemed to narrow, focus on her forehead, and stab at her like a blade of cold, black obsidian. Oldest Death's gaze didn't stop there. It reached inward, and spread downward toward her center.

Shivering, she began as best she could, "So, I, uh …" That was as far as she got.

The dark and cold and, she imagined, anger of his consciousness bored an icy hole down into her very essence.

"Uh," she tried again.

"Please," Oldest Death said. "Skip the journey. First timers always want to recount the journey. I have a suicide bomb in Ankara to attend to."

He knew exactly what she'd been about to do. Flustered, she said, "Yes. Of course."

"And don't babble."

"Um. Well."

"Walk with me." He turned and strode along the river of lives toward the mixed mess of metaphors that made up the Middle East. "Sometimes that helps."

Relieved that he no longer peered down into her, she jogged to catch up, tripped on her robes, gathered them, and scrambled to move up beside him.

He moved quickly and surely into the tangled mess of the middle-eastern soul delta.

"There was a family grieving," she said.

"Really?"

"Oh," she said. "Maybe they were there for the other child."

"How many?"

"Two. Two children."

"No. The family."

"Oh. Sorry." She stumbled.

"Well?"

She quick-stepped to catch up. "Three. Parents and sibling."

"Parents? Man and woman?"

"Uh-huh. Yeah. And the machines beeped. The room was small. There were toys."

He stopped. Without looking at her, he asked, "What kind?"

"I don't know. Breathing things? Heart things?"

Coldly, he said, "Not the machines. The toys."

She tried to be casual, like she did this sort of thing all the time. "The usual. Electrical padtops, blocks, raggedy dolls, color books, a card game, and—"

"And," Oldest Death interrupted. Somehow impossibly colder and darker, he said, "You played with the toys."

Knowing she couldn't lie about it, she murmured, "A little." Before he spoke again, she said, "You know, while I waited."

To her relief, he began to walk again. "Which toys?"

"Mostly the cards."

"Who played *cards* with you?"

This confused her. She hadn't played cards before, so she didn't know anything about other people playing. "Nobody," she managed.

"Solitaire, then?"

"Yeah. It was a game about travelling in the underworld." she said, "Not our Underworld. It was all wrong for that. It was all curses and blessings and dragons and trolls—magical story stuff. I mean, when I started, I didn't think I'd like it, but once I got the—"

He stopped again.

Her feet and mouth froze.

He turned to face her.

She once again had his icy, undivided attention.

"You gathered the soul?"

"Yes, Sir."

His voice seemed to warm a little, and he walked on. “And delivered it to the lake?”

“Yes, Sir.”

“Good.”

In her relief, she relaxed, dropped the hem of her robes, and immediately tripped on them. The Cur of Crisis darted in front of her, and she caught herself on his thick shoulders. She didn’t think Oldest Death saw her trip.

He went on, “And the soul returned to the cycle of Overworld and Underworld.”

She stayed where she was, steadying herself on the dog.

Oldest moved on for two long, dark, cold strides.

She murmured, “I guess.”

Now, Oldest froze. He didn’t have to turn to face her. The icy obsidian knife stabbed into her forehead again.

“You *guess*?”

“It was my first one.” She hated herself for making it sound like an excuse before he had discovered her mistake. She gambled what little she knew about him and the job against the sharp tone of his voice. “Well,” she said, “it wasn’t like it was a special soul or anything.”

Now, he turned, and his gaze made her smaller than the tiniest bacterium spark at the very bottom of her bucket and colder and more terrified than she had ever been in the Marianas Deeps bucketing up spark sludge from single-celled sea creatures.

"Oh," Oldest Death said. "The soul wasn't special at all?"

Terrified to speak and sure she had just trapped herself, she willed herself to stand very still and silent.

Three Horror Hound heads whimpered at once. The dog fell over and rolled on its back.

She hoped Oldest Death didn't speak Doom Puppy. If he did, she hoped the Dark Dog of Deception wouldn't say anything to get her put back on full-time bucket duty.

After what seemed like two eternities slogging heavy buckets of mold and bacteria souls to the lake, Oldest Death turned away and continued toward the carnage of the Middle East. "Good work," he said. "I'll add you to the rotation for 21st Century America."

She'd been about to tell him about the brightness, the walking on the lake surface, the branch, chalice, and transcendence, but she swallowed the words and bit her own dead tongue.

Oldest Death slipped through a shadow into Overworld and was gone.

The silvery-blue glow of souls flowing in the Middle East mosaic delta and returning to flesh in Overworld cast her shadow up the rocky shore and against a black wall. She imagined that her shadow was taller and that she had grown, so why did she feel so small inside?

The three-headed Child of Kerberos, Protector of the Realm of Hades, licked her bony hand with Left's mouth and nestled Center's head under her fingernails for a scratch. Automatically, she dug in. "That was close," she said.

Center moaned his pleasure.

Left tried to push him away and take over the reflexively scratching hand.

Center wasn't having it.

"We need to fix this," Littlest Death said.

She was dead sure she had screwed up. The only problem was that she still wasn't entirely sure what she had done wrong or what would fix it.

Backtracking

Sitting on the thinking rock in her thinking place, Littlest Death thought. She tossed another pebble into the lake.

Littlest Kerberos lunged forward, as if to give chase, but he stopped at the edge of the lake as if the viscous, silvery fluid might be too cold. Of course, that wasn't it. Barking Banshee just knew better than to enter the Lake of All Souls.

That was the way to the flesh. Most Underworlders instinctively knew it was just not a good idea to jump in the lake. He might be a death dog, but who knew what the Lake of All Souls would do to him.

Littlest Death had never ventured into the lake. No death had, as far as she knew. Nobody had forbad her from doing it, but it just, well, felt *wrong*.

Apparently, it felt wrong to Guardian Growlers, too.

The ripples from her stone expanded like they always did. They lapped gently against the shore like they always did. She tossed another stone.

In her mind, she went over and over what she had done, trying to see what had gone wrong. She tried to tell herself that any soul transcending had to be good, so delivering a soul to the moment of transcendence had to be okay. If it wasn't okay, then all the legends about it were lies. If it wasn't okay, then the whole idea of the Lake of Souls had to be …

Well, she didn't want to think about that possibility after a thousand years of hauling buckets of slime sparks. That would be, well … It would be …

No. No. No.

Something was wrong, but it wasn't the Lake of All Souls. It wasn't the soul's transcendence.

Her conversation with Oldest Death made it very clear she had not been intended to carry a transcendent soul. She remembered what the soul had said as they traveled into and through Underworld. It had remembered its lives before, and it had remembered Azrael's name and the path to the lake. It had even talked about meeting its Uncle Lawrence last time.

Remembering wasn't normal, but it transcended. Maybe it was normal for souls on their way up and out. It had to be.

She tried to shake off her doubt by skipping back in her mind to the moment at which she had gathered in the soul.

The soul was ready. It saw her. Only souls that were ready could see deaths.

The machine beeped. The doctors ran in. She lifted the soul out of the flesh and returned it to Underworld.

Nothing was wrong in any of that, but Oldest Death had implied that she had been sent for a normal soul. Nobody she talked to admitted to having seen a transcendent soul before, but somebody must have or there wouldn't be any stories about them.

She tossed a pebble up on the shore for Triple Threat. He dutifully retrieved it, each head fighting for possession right up until she took it from Right's mouth. Absently, she tossed it again. Right delivered again.

Again.

Center.

Again.

Left.

Lost in thought, she lost track of her Howling Hound head count.

When no Death Doggie Noggin delivered the tossed stone, she looked for the mutt. He had plopped down a ways up the shore and gone to sleep. Looking at his peaceful heads all lolled and sleeping, it struck her that expecting the dog to be there when she reached for the stone was like expecting to find answers in her memories. The problem might not be in her memories. It might be where her memories weren't.

Maybe the problem happened before she lifted the soul, but she couldn't imagine where or how.

Oldest Death had seemed upset about her playing the card game, but the cards couldn't have influenced the soul. That was just silly. He had also been surprised about the grieving family.

Maybe something in the hospital was an influence.

And there was the little girl's soul she had seen before entering the room. Maybe Azrael could help. As usual, he had been bright, righteous, winged, abrupt, and tired. As usual, he had still managed to silence down his nose at her.

But he might know something she didn't. He might be able to help.

Before she had gotten ten yards, the Three-Headed Apocalypse had playfully tangled her robes, knocked her to the ground, and given her face a three-tongue bath.

Azrael

She had been right. Azrael remembered seeing her. Coldly, he congratulated her on her first human.

She said a hurried thank you.

Azrael, like most of the metaphor-locked deaths, played his meta character perfectly. Unlike some of the angels, Azrael served three of Earth's major belief systems. She found him kneeling on a stone *prie-dieu*, bright wings folded behind him and glowing face turned upward to the blinding light at the top of the cavern beyond the river Lethe, where he sometimes stood guard when not retrieving souls. Hands held flat together in supplication, he murmured prayers that Littlest was grateful she had never had to learn in order to gather the sparks of germs and fungi.

Between lines of prayer, Azrael spoke. "I remember you passing us."

"And going into the room," she said.

"No. We left before that."

"Think hard."

"I don't have to think. I have faith."

"I need help," she said.

"Pray with me, Child."

"Will it help?"

"Humans think it does, so I do it."

"So, no." This wasn't getting her anywhere.

In a heavy, tired voice, he said, "It would be nice to not have to do it alone for once."

She glanced up at the brilliant light above and considered kneeling next to him. It couldn't hurt.

Instead, she said, "Something strange happened, and I don't understand it."

Clearly disappointed that she hadn't knelt, he said, "Tell Oldest Death."

"He's busy in the Middle East."

Azrael crossed himself, kissed his thumb, and touched his forehead. "Ha'Elohim haggadol. All praise to God. Allahu Akbar."

"Uh. Yeah." Humans were complicated. Maybe she'd just go find her bucket and go back to—

Azrael interrupted her thought by saying, "Amen," standing, turning, and stretching his bright wings out to their full twenty-foot span.

She had to admit he was impressive, but it also had to be awkward in narrow caverns. She wondered if they worked in Overworld or if they were just meta-props like Baast's Ankh necklace.

He folded them back up and said, "Here's what I remember. I picked up Sarah from the cancer ward. She was very scared, so I was her personal angel for a while. We sat and chatted with some of the other kids who were close enough to death to be able to see us. We talked afterlife and love and how easy it is once you let go of the flesh."

Impatient, she interrupted him. "Yeah, but my soul was in a room alone with one other child."

Azrael started. His beatific glow dimmed a bit, and she thought he was going to silence down his nose at her, but he asked, "Which other child?"

"I don't know," she said. "There was a family. There were two kids in the room, a boy and a girl. I brought out the boy."

This seemed to upset Azrael. "His name?"

"I didn't ask."

"You took a human soul, and you don't even know his name?"

"I never had to know names before."

"Every creature is blessed, but humans are not bugs." Now, Azrael definitely silenced down his nose at her.

She hated that. Oh, she hated that. "Seriously? I mean, really? You want to soul shame me? Like you remember the name of every soul you've ever pulled into Underworld?"

His glow returned and he smiled. "Already picking up 21st century American idiom?"

She didn't like the smug way he said it, but when an angel smiles, pretty much anything and everything capable of smiling just lights up and smiles along.

She still didn't like it.

"What's the big deal?" she said. "I know he had an uncle named Lawrence in his last life."

He stopped smiling and dimmed again. "The big deal is that you left a soul in dying flesh."

"She isn't dead."

"Oh, for the love of—" Azrael stopped himself, crossed himself, and said, "Mea Culpa, mea culpa, mea maxima culpa."

Littlest watched the angel dim and the grave look on his face. The horror of what he had said hit her. The flesh would die, but the soul would be trapped within. That had never mattered to her before. She could just come back for the spark of a bacteria later.

But a child's soul trapped in dying flesh—

Fixing It

Littlest Death ran, robes fluttering behind her. The Divine Death Dog followed, leaping and snapping at her fluttering robes. Tripping on her hem and trying to gather the robes ahead of her while slapping at the robes behind her to keep the pup from dragging her back, she pushed with all her spectral strength toward the rivulet that lead to the hospital.

Bursting forth into Overworld and leaving the Demidog of Whining behind, she halted to get her bearings.

The hospital hadn't changed.

It was the same bright place full of busy people moving here and there, sad and anxious people waiting, and smells of clean and sick intermingling. A disembodied voice said calm things over a PA system.

Several blank deaths and a couple of metas moved about purposefully and unseen among the humans. She hoped they didn't recognize her. Pulling her cowl up and around her face, she went up on toes to try look taller as she hurried to the room where the card game had caused so much trouble.

The little group of three people sat on a cushioned bench seat outside the room. The woman held the boy. The man held the woman. All three shuddered, gasped, and suppressed sobs.

Grief over the child she had taken.

She had certainly known that it happened, but she hadn't really seen it before. They all looked like it hurt—a lot. The little family was in terrible pain. She had once seen that look of fatal, sad resignation on the face of a fawn trapped by a pack of wolves.

Then, she'd been excited because she was the only death around and would get to pull in the soul of a mammal.

Then, a First Nations meta, a large blue butterfly, had landed on the fawn and lifted its soul to help it handle the change to Underworld. Littlest had taken her bucket back to the little swamp where she'd been working.

Each face in the human family looked like the fawn.

She glanced about, looking for the death or deaths who would come to claim their souls. At least for the moment, the corridor was empty of her kind. She slipped past the family and into the room.

Time in Underworld moved differently than time in the world of flesh. In Underworld, time moved in circles and bent to the will of each and all. She had done so much since she left this stark room, but only a few minutes seemed to have passed. The doctors and nurses still worked frantically on the empty body.

Otherwise, the room was the same. The little table of toys sat undisturbed against the wall. The toy car underneath still hid from human view. The other bed still held a very sick girl.

The girl's machine made a continuous, electronic tone.

The doctors had not noticed yet, but they had turned off the boy's machine.

The poor soul in the sick child was trapped. While the doctors worked, the soul in the shell of the hairless girl lifted its head free of the flesh, opened her wide, glowing eyes, and stared in pleading silence at Littlest Death.

Without Littlest's help, the poor girl had been there, flesh-bound and suffering, for how long?

Minutes, Littlest imagined, but every death knew that kind of suffering could damage a soul—even turn it dark and ugly. A soul trapped in dying flesh lived tortured eternities in each tiny slice of time.

Time.

She knew what she had to do, and she stepped up to the poor child.

"I'm so sorry," Littlest said.

She reached out to the child's hand, touched it, and took the soul's hand in her own. The soul lifted gently from the flesh. As it came free, the pained and sallow face of the dying child relaxed. A single, final sigh escaped the flesh's lips, and the girl's spirit came free. Beside Littlest Death, the released soul stood whole—relieved of weight and pain.

The soul looked at the lifeless body in the bed. "That sucked," she said.

"I'm sorry. I should have come for you sooner."

The child seemed to notice Littlest Death for the first time. "Oh," she said. "Weren't you just here?"

Littlest nodded. "I took the other one."

"It's okay," the girl said. "I'm glad you came back. I'm not sure how much more of that I could have taken."

One of the doctors said, "Turn off the monitor."

A nurse said, "I did."

A man near the foot of the bed moved over to the two machines. "Doctor," he said. "The girl."

The white-coated woman who seemed to be in charge cursed loudly.

The door opened, and the man from the hall, tears still on his cheeks, looked in.

The woman ordered, "Get him out of here."

The nurse barked, "Yes, Doctor," spread her arms wide, and moved toward the man. He tried to dodge, but the woman knew her job. She intercepted him.

"Paul? Baby?" the man said.

While the first nurse moved the boy's father back into the hall, a second nurse went to a speaker on the wall, pressed a button, and called for help. "Code Blue. Dr. Tiny, 327 double."

The little soul next to Littlest said, "That means two people are dying in the children's ward."

"They should just say that," Littlest Death said.

"Mommies and Daddies get upset," the freshly freed soul said. "It happens a lot. This is a busy place."

"We should go," Littlest said.

"What about Paul?"

"Paul?"

The little girl soul pointed to the body of the boy Littlest had taken earlier. "He was supposed to get better."

"He's gone," Littlest said.

"He said he was going to be okay."

"We can't help him," Littlest said.

Matter-of-factly, the new soul said, "Well, that's not right."

Littlest Death wasn't sure what to say. There was no point in explaining to a fresh little girl's soul that a death had screwed up. Instead, Littlest said, "Everyone has to go."

As soon as she said it, it felt wrong. That boy didn't have to go. Littlest Death had taken him. She wanted to apologize to the father, to Oldest, to the girl by her side—to someone.

"Not Paul," the new girl said. "He was sure. Look at his Dad."

Littlest Death did look.

The nurse had almost pushed the man out of the room, but the man deftly twisted, side-stepped, and slipped past her.

His face was terrible to look at—twisted, pale, angry, and terrified all at once.

Littlest Death had never seen such a face. His mouth was open like he was screaming, but he wasn't screaming. He barely breathed at all. Water poured from his eyes—black pupils set in wide, white circles filled with rage and pain.

Littlest Death turned away and tugged on the girl's hand. She couldn't worry about the father, the mother, or the sibling. She had to get the right soul back to the Lake of All Souls. She couldn't fix anything here. She had to make her mistake right in Underworld.

The little soul held back and said, "It's so sad."

"It's always sad," Littlest Death offered, pulling the girl toward the hallways.

The little girl said, "Paul had a good family. He was going to be something good—someone who helped the world."

Littlest Death didn't want to hear such things. She just didn't. She wanted to get out of the room, down the hall, and safely through the veil.

Every human died. It wasn't bad. The boy was gone. He had transcended. Transcendence *couldn't* be bad.

She dragged the little girl along.

The little girl pulled back, but Littlest was too strong for the child soul.

The memory of Azrael tugging his child toward the veil came to her. She'd thought him mean and thought herself better. Now, she wondered if he just knew a few things about helping children to the lake that she didn't.

The child scrambled to keep up.

They moved around and through the hustling, hurrying people in the hallways.

"Will I get to see him?" the girl asked.

"Who?"

"Paul."

The girl kept up, but she wouldn't stop talking. Littlest Death just wanted her to be quiet.

"Is he an angel now?"

"No," Littlest Death said.

"Sure he is," the little girl said. "He was special. Everybody could see that."

It just kept getting worse. Littlest Death hadn't seen it.

The little soul said, "I'm sure he's an angel now."

"He's gone. That's all. He's just gone."

Littlest had taken a soul that had been meant to help people move forward, become more, grow, and be the best souls they could be. She had killed a prophet or a healer or a saint. Littlest Death didn't know what Paul was supposed to be, but she knew he wasn't supposed to be dead yet.

"I wish I could do something for his Dad," the girl said.

And it came to Littlest Death that maybe the new soul could.

Almost to the veil in the shadows at the end of a hallway, she froze.

Doctors and nurses and orderlies moved around them like urgent shadows made of flesh and bone.

Littlest Death turned to the girl and said, "Do you understand what will happen to you now? Have you been to the lake before?"

The soul peered into her cowl much the way Oldest Death had peered except that the girl's gaze didn't fill Littlest with ice and a terror of being seen right down into the deepest and darkest fearful, secret place at her core. After a long moment, the little girl blinked, sort of flickered, and said, "I think I have." The little soul seemed to glow suddenly brighter. The girl smiled. "I get it. Awesomesauce! Can you do it?"

"I think so." Littlest Death wasn't sure, but she had to try. She had made this mess, and she could fix it. "Can you? I mean, be what you need to be?"

The little girl soul nodded. "I think so."

Together, they turned back.

Holding the soul's hand, they passed Paul's terrified family and entered the room again. Both beds were surrounded by sweating, stern, scared doctors and nurses frantically trying to save both children.

Littlest Death helped the little girl's soul up onto Paul's bed and into the body of the dead boy.

As she tucked the happy little soul into the inanimate flesh, she did her best to reach out, to feel it connect to new flesh. She wanted so badly for it to connect, to bond, to become a whole child on the bed.

The little girl wanted it, too. Her soul burned almost as bright as Paul's had.

Littlest Death imagined that the little girl's soul had already risen from the flesh, moved with Littlest into Underworld, travelled upstream to the lake, mingled with the loving experiences of a million other souls, returned to the rivers, and once again found Overworld and flesh—this flesh.

With all her heart, Littlest imagined the opposite of what she had done earlier. She imagined the moment when a soul flowed into a body and ignited life.

A sudden flash of ethereal light erupted in the room and blinded her.

When she could see again, the girl's soul had released her hand and completely immersed itself in the flesh of Paul's body.

Someone said, "I have a heartbeat."

The doctor said, “Turn on the monitor.”

One of the machines chirped rapidly then settled into a rhythm.

The Paul body gasped, twisted its head away from the mask a nurse held over nose and mouth. Dead, gray eyelids flushed pink and opened. The deep brown eyes rolled and focused on Littlest Death.

Littlest hadn’t known what to expect, but she hadn’t expected that. She slipped back away from the bed toward the wall, the table, and the Ace of Cups.

Whispered words came from Paul’s mouth. “I’m here. Thank you.”

“Vitals stable,” a nurse said.

Someone said, “Thank God.”

Someone else said, “Stay with him. The rest of you, help the girl.”

While the doctors and nurses shifted from Paul’s side to either help the girl who was not coming back or to leave the room, Paul’s father slipped to the side of the bed next to his son. He took up the tiny hand and squeezed it.

The little girl’s face—no—Paul’s face turned from Littlest Death to his new/old father. The boy smiled and squeezed back.

Littlest Death wondered how the father’s face could have changed so little and so much in a few short moments.

The man’s mouth still gaped. Tears still flowed. However, she felt no horror from him, no terror, rage, or pain.

The man seemed exhausted and elated—almost drunk on joy.

She told herself she'd think about that later. What mattered now was the right body had a soul. She'd taken one and left one. It added up.

A million souls in a bucket had never been as much trouble as one in a bed.

Exhausted, she slipped away and back to Underworld where the Three-headed Terrier of Terror waited for her to toss stones and play robe tug. Littlest thought she might like to have her face licked while she hugged the dog. Yes. That would be just about the perfect thing.

New Assignment

It didn't take her long to navigate the caverns and rivers of Underworld. She didn't even try to ditch the Triple-tongued Threat.

Together, they encountered other deaths. Some had heard of her having taken her first human soul. Some of those congratulated her. A couple pointedly ignored her—metas.

When they chanced upon Baast, she smiled a knowing cat's smile and said something cryptic. "A beginning is an ending is your beginning."

Littlest was beginning to like canine guardians of the underworld more than felines. Dogs were straight-forward. Even when they had three heads, you could pretty well predict their moods and what they wanted. Throw a stone. Chase a stone. Run away. Chase robes. Once, she had tossed a stone and seen Anubis flinch as if he wanted to chase it. To the credit of his dignity, he did not. But she could have sworn for a second there …

Not cats.

Littlest Death wanted to ask what Baast meant, but Littlest was still too afraid of anyone finding out about the transcendent soul and the soul shuffle at the hospital. While it seemed silly to take a perfectly good soul out of Overworld, dump it in the lake, and wait for it to get back to Overworld to enter a body, she was pretty sure it was against whatever rules existed to just pull a soul and put it in another body without bringing it to Underworld and the lake first. She'd certainly never heard any stories about it being done.

So, she pretended she had succeeded. She pretended she understood human souls. While she pretended, a huge sense of relief washed over her when she took her bucket in search of mold souls, fungi souls, and a few million krill sparks.

Hades Puppy tagged along.

Between dumping full buckets, she tossed rocks. He retrieved. She ran. He chased.

Nothing to see here. Meta or blank, just move along. Everything is normal. Right?

Focused and diligent in her normalcy, she even learned to toss three rocks at once so all three heads could come back proud and happy—except when Left took two stones and left Center without one. Center had the hardest time getting a stone because it was pretty much inevitable that the end heads, Left and Right, would get to a tossed rock first.

It took Littlest Death a few tries at creating stone fetching equality to figure out why. Apparently, all three heads tried to guide the body at once. If she tossed three stones, each head picked a stone. Sometimes, two picked the same stone, but all three rarely picked the same stone, so the body tended to move on sporadic curves that brought the edge heads to the targets first.

So, she finally compensated by tossing four rocks. That gave Left two rocks every time.

Center and Right didn't seem to mind, and Left could be more proud than the others. Every head was happy, and it kept Littlest Death busy and visible as the harmless, inconsequential death she wanted the others to think she still was.

Inconsequential. Those were the days.

Taking the two stones from happy Left, she said, "Pride will be your undoing, you know."

She couldn't tell if he understood her because the tail wagged exactly the same as if he hadn't. Center and Right seemed oblivious to the obvious deficiency in Left's ethical makeup.

Eventually, the deaths were called once more to the Arena.

"I wonder," Littlest Death asked all three heads of the Dark Doggie while they walked together, "if you will grow up and replace your father?"

Then, because she couldn't get Paul, the little girl, and the family out of her mind, another thought occurred to her. "Did you have a mother? A brother or sister?"

Center yipped, as if to say Littlest Death had asked a stupid question. Center often seemed to have a better grasp of things than either Right or Left. Littlest suspected that was because Center had to think harder in order to get food and retrieve stones. Left and Right could leave a certain amount of their good fortune to chance.

They arrived at the arched path into the Arena of Assignments. Littlest Death led the Dire Hound off to one side of the arch. "Sit," she commanded.

To her surprise, all three heads seemed attentive and the body sat without shivering, shaking, or spinning in a circle first.

"Well," she said. "That's an improvement."

Center yipped.

Right whimpered and mooned sad, "don't go in there and leave us," eyes.

Left nodded and seemed to beam his pride in his righteous obedience.

"Stay." She lifted one bony hand, hoping to put some authority into her halt gesture, but her dark sleeve flounced over her palm.

The Hades Hound didn't seem to mind.

"I think I'll get assigned another human," she said.

Only Left seemed to agree with her.

"I'm pretty sure," she said.

Center shook his head and made his ears slap against his cheeks.

"Nobody knows," she said, but the heads had already lost interest. Each looked in a different direction, and none paid attention to her.

She left the Demented Dingo and went into the arena to get her assignment. She hoped it would be another human. She'd do much better now that she knew what to expect. All the stories in the world, she told herself, hadn't really prepared her for the toys, for the machines, for the family, for grief, and especially not for transcendence.

It was too overwhelming the first time.

Now that she had let the experience settle in, she could do better. She'd just focus really hard. She'd make sure she had the right soul. She'd ask its name. If she had to, she would trace the wires from the bodies to the machines and make sure she had the right machine and the right body and the right soul.

And she absolutely would not play Dungeon Solitaire.

She could do it.

In the arena, Oldest Death handed out the assignments again. He even handed out assignments for fungi and Marianas sludge sparks to unhappy blanks, and that made her feel all the more excited. If he was using other deaths for the bucket jobs, maybe he had something special in mind for her.

One-by-one, the other deaths received their assignments and went off to fulfill their duties. Death-by-death, the arena emptied.

Little-by-little, she became more and more nervous.

Finally, the last death had gone and she was alone, nervous, and facing Oldest Death. She hoped he couldn't see her shaking under her robes.

He said, "I have something special in mind for you, Littlest Death."

Relief flooded through her. She'd been right.

Something special!

She jumped up. Then, she realized she didn't want to look too excited. She tried to show the proper respect by bowing her head, but she felt like she only succeeded in flipping her cowl about.

Oh, how she hoped she would grow into her robes soon.

"I'm ready," she said.

Suddenly, that feeling that he was looking into her, through her, and beyond her into the future of her existence and every hidden moment of her past chilled her.

She had his undivided attention again.

"No," he said. "You are not, but I have little choice."

The idea that Oldest Death had limited choices was new to her. He was the oldest and most experienced death in Underworld, and she had always assumed that he, more than any other creature, had infinite choices.

"I don't understand," she said.

"You do, but you pretend that you don't."

The chill of his gaze expanded inside her until she felt like a death-shaped ice statue. She did understand.

He knew.

"Yes," he said. "I know."

"Baast?" she asked. She couldn't believe Baast knew. Even if Baast did know, she wouldn't have reported it. At least, Littlest didn't think she would have.

Oldest Death shook his hood.

"Ereshkigal?"

"No, Little One."

"Who?"

"I am Oldest Death," he said. "I have numbered the souls of the universe and watched over them since the first spark of the first life in the first puddle of ooze needed gathering. I gathered that spark. I placed it in the chalice held by the hand on the branch of the tree of life. I watched it trickle slowly down the branch and across the dry lake bed and along cracks and gullies in the new and cooling stone of Underworld until it found its way to Overworld and a new accumulation of slime and enzymes and oddly organized molecules again."

She gasped at the endlessness and enormity of what he had just said. "All the souls?"

"All of them."

Shame and guilt swept through her like the river of souls flows forever toward life. After a long pause, she whispered, "I should have told you."

"You should have, but it made no difference."

"Fungi and paramecia, then." She kicked at a pebble but got her toe caught in her robe. "Forever? Please, not forever."

"No, Littlest Death."

So, she had some hope. "I'll work hard," she said. "Maybe in a thousand years, you'll—"

"Look at me," he said.

She looked up. "Punishment?"

"No."

Confused, she asked, "Nothing?"

"There were two souls. One, you retrieved before his time, but he was, none-the-less, ready to transcend the worlds, so he did."

She nodded. "I couldn't stop him."

"Nor should you have tried. That would have been much worse."

"The other," she said, "is in the body left by the ascended soul."

"Yes," he said. "And that will do nicely, I think. She was well developed, and she will learn much from being thrust into Paul's role as a healer of living souls. It will be harder for the second soul, but I believe she will rise to the duty of attending to the needs of others. After all, she saw the father's pain and responded with love."

Littlest Death thought she could hear the rustle of her robes echoing off the empty, curved tiers of the arena. Finally, terrified of the punishment that might come in the answer, she said, "What, then?"

Oldest Death put a long-boned hand on her shoulder and said, "Make it right."

"I did my best."

"Yes. Now, do better."

She said, "The right body died. You said the girl's soul in Paul's body would be okay."

"Yes," he said, "but you still have a missing soul."

Frustrated and a little scared, she pleaded, "How?"

Oldest Death had no face, so she couldn't see his mouth, but she thought perhaps he smiled as he said, "The soul you did not bring back to Underworld did not enter the Lake of All Souls. It did not flow along its new river, along its new stream, and ultimately make the passage into new life."

"I don't understand."

"Exactly."

She stared. Realization hit her.

Of course.

Somewhere, a baby was born without a soul. That couldn't be good, but she had no idea what she could do about it.

"Pride," he said. "You believed you understood, but you did not. Because you believed you understood, you could not experience what was needed to bring understanding."

Confused, she looked for something safe to say—something that would get her away from Oldest Death and, if possible, out of the arena. She said, "What should I do?"

"In Overworld, a soulless child has been born. Go to the soulless child. Set things right." Oldest Death squeezed her shoulder gently, turned her toward the arched path out of the arena, and pushed her away.

She thought she might collapse beneath his kind hand, but she knew she could not. She stumbled forward, got her feet under her, and took a hesitant step on her own.

He had waited until the others were gone to tell her he knew. He had let her know what she must do without humiliating her in front of others.

She turned back. "There's another soul I must find," she said.

"Yes."

"You know where." She stated it.

"Yes."

"And you won't tell me."

He pointed toward the arched exit to the arena.

She found nothing in his featureless face, so she turned and trudged away from Oldest Death. With every step, his cold gaze bored into her back. She was sure he was angry, sad, stern, and amused. She also felt something else—something unexpected—joy and certainty.

He believed in her.

She had never before suspected that he held anything but indifference, or maybe contempt, toward her, but she had felt his kindness and belief in his grip and gaze.

Oldest Death believed she could set things right, and he wanted her to do it herself and without his help or anyone else's.

So, she would.

She lifted her robes and strode forward with more confidence.

She would fix her mistake, and she would come back to him and tell him, and thank him for his wisdom and kindness. Then, she'd be a real death, and nobody could question it.

Puppy of Playfulness was still sitting and staying, which she took to be a good omen. If there were miracles, three heads all agreeing to keep one body still was a big one. If one miracle could happen, perhaps others could.

An Answer

In the circular foreverness of Underworld, a river can split into streams and streams into creeks and creeks into rivulets flowing an inch or a mile in seconds or in millennia of the time measured in Overworld. Each tiny trickle of soul can, and will, find its place without guidance.

If fact, Littlest Death had been told that each soul chose its point of return based on what it knew that it needed to learn, deep inside its heart of all knowings. For a soul returned to the Lake of All Souls, finding the way along the watershed of spirit into flesh was a simple thing.

For Littlest Death, who had screwed up the natural order, finding the absence of a soul in the Lake of All Souls and then following that *never been there soul* along the many splits and forks of ever decreasing silver, living light was impossible.

It would have been impossible for any death. They just weren't built for following missing life into Overworld.

For days, for weeks, for years, for ages, she searched the paths of the rivers for the place the soul had not gone.

She searched, but she didn't find—couldn't find.

She tried to train the Three-Snouted Monster to sniff for empty flesh at the edges of Overworld beside the tiniest of rivulets of soul where they disappeared from Underworld.

They found nothing—nothing at all.

That was the problem. They were looking for nothing—an emptiness. It was like trying to find a shadow in the dark.

Time circled. She and her friend failed.

So, she sat on her worn rock, pebble in hand, and the growing, warm bulk of the Dauntless Dog propping up her back. Staring at the silvery surface of the Lake of All Souls, she let her mind wander aimlessly, unaware of the three cocked heads and the six intent, fiery eyes focused on the pebble in her hand.

He had grown, but he wasn't yet a true hound. Still a puppy, his paws were the size of her head and still seemed too big for him. She extended a bony finger and poked one of his paws.

He pulled it back.

She held the stone out in her palm for him. Center poked it with his nose, but neither Left nor Right made a move to pick it up. All three wanted her to throw it.

She feigned a toss over her shoulder.

Both edge heads jerked back to follow the arc of the stone that had not been thrown.

Center still focused on her hand, but it didn't matter. Left and Right dragged whining Center away to search for the nothing she had thrown into the cavernous shadows.

Once the Monster With Three Brains was gone, she tossed the pebble, like so many others before, into the silvery shimmer of the lake. It plopped into the glowing liquid of life. Ripples spread outward from the stone.

Their rolling, expanding progress soothed her. Moments passed, and the gentle lapping of the tiny waves against the shore at her feet reminded her of endless, careless hours sitting just there doing just that.

One soul, she thought. Why was it such a big deal? She had poured millions upon millions of sparks into the lake. One soul out of place was nothing. One empty body couldn't matter when compared to the millions and millions she had retrieved.

She remembered the beauty of Paul's transcendence—the calm and certainty and bliss of his walking and rising.

Then, the tortured face of Paul's father came to mind.

One soul mattered. One soul made a difference.

She might have poured millions into the lake, but she had also seen with her own eyes the power of just one, brilliant, illuminated, transcendent soul.

One soul *was* something—one soul immersed in the lake and part of the lake. It touched all the other souls—all of them at once, and Oldest Death could touch every single one.

His amazing awareness of so many had seemed impossible to her. She couldn't do it, so she had believed nobody could.

She thought it impossible to find what wasn't, either. She believed that couldn't be done.

Oldest Death believed it could.

She tossed another stone.

The ripples expanded and lapped at the shore.

The Terrier of Terror pushed against her shoulder. The edge heads had apparently given in to Center.

She scratched Center behind the ears. "My friend," she said. "You're always with me."

Center pushed his forehead hard against her chest so she could get better leverage for her scratching. Left and Right hadn't yet noticed that Center was getting a lot of attention. They still seemed uncertain about having lost the stone that wasn't in the shadows.

She pressed her face into Center's fur and gave up. No matter what Oldest Death believed, she was like Left and Right. It just wasn't possible to find nothing in emptiness.

Scratching the dog and content in the thoughtless, emptiness of accepting her failure, the answer came to her like a star exploding at the end of its life.

It had been so simple.

She jumped up, kissed Center on the nose, and ran along the shore.

Left, Right, and Center all caught her excitement and raced after her.

She'd been looking for what wasn't there—a not soul in the river on its way to a body with no soul. She and the Canine of Calamity had searched every veil and path to Overworld, seeking an empty shell.

The dog was always with her. The dog always knew where she was. Even when she was in Overworld, it somehow knew where she would be when she stepped back into Underworld. It was like it could smell her emotions—her joy, fear, sadness, or excitement. It always seemed to know how she felt.

The parents and Paul's brother were like the dog.

In their hearts, they always knew. They grieved, however briefly, when his flesh was empty.

She had felt it.

They danced in joy when the girl's soul came into Paul's flesh.

She didn't have to find the empty flesh. She had to find the grief of the family of a child born without a soul.

The Empty Vessel

Littlest Death began her search again.

The Morte d' Mongrel followed at her heels, nipping and snapping at the flutter and flow of robes. She had learned to run without slapping back at the heads and billowing robes, or maybe she had gotten a little taller. It wasn't like she had a human family who measured her height against a wall or door arch. She was what she was and, as far as it mattered, she was what she had always been.

Littlest Death started near the hospital where everything had gone wrong. There, just inside the veil between Underworld and the hospital, she grabbed Center in both hands, pulled his face close, and did her best to peer right into his head the way Oldest peered into hers. "Find the grief," she said. "Hunt it up."

Left and Right both chuffed.

Right yipped.

She released the Hunting Hound, and all three heads turned as one. The body followed, and they were off at a run.

Up the river of life, through cavern after cavern, they ran. One head would dip to scent the ground. One would rise and sniff the air. The other would howl. The heads went up, down, and up, but they never slowed the pace.

Once, she stopped and moved along a tiny rivulet toward a hospital veil. She thought it might lead them to a newborn child. After all, it seemed reasonable to seek a newborn in a maternity ward, but the Dog of Death, Destruction, and Mayhem seemed to think it was the wrong branch of the tiniest of rivulets of the glowing silver tendrils of flowing soul.

He seemed to understand what she wanted, and all three heads agreed and pointed along another rivulet to her left.

That agreement was rare enough to catch her attention, so she veered left at the last, tiniest twist in the glowing rivulets.

She broke through into Overworld in a dark corridor. She knew it wasn't a hospital because it didn't have the smell of forced cleanliness overlaying illness, nor did she feel the pull of souls hoping for release, and pretty much all hospitals felt that way. After all, hadn't she been to thousands of facilities to pick up the tiny sparks from the many one-celled bodies that died every day under the onslaught of cleaning products and medicines?

The Hound of Hope had, of course, remained in Underworld, so she couldn't rely on his nose and instincts.

Instead, she gathered her robes and, excited in spite of so little hope of success, hurried along the dark hallway.

Each door she came to, she pressed through.

Each room she entered was empty and unkempt. She discovered dust-covered, velvet and walnut furniture—Victorian, she thought.

She didn't think it likely she had come through into an earlier age. It did happen that a soul returned to flesh in an earlier era because the circumstances in that time would teach what it needed, but she had a strange feeling this soul would return to 21st Century United States.

She had never given such things much thought before. Except for Paul, the little girl, a lizard, two rats, and a platypus, she had only chased the tiniest of sparks leaving the flesh.

Curiosity mixed with her sense of urgency, and she overruled her doubts and justified entering another room, and another, telling herself that a few more rooms wouldn't matter one way or the other.

After ten rooms, all pretty much the same, she decided the dog was a stupid way to choose a path into Overworld. Oldest Death would never have followed a dog. Three heads did not make a Greek Chorus Hound any smarter than one. If anything, three heads just confused matters.

To nobody in particular, she said, "There's a reason most creatures in Overworld only have one head—one head; one soul; one mind."

Just before she turned to make her way back into Underworld, a familiar sound stopped her. It came from the end of the hallway—the gentle lapping of ripples against the stone edges of the Lake of All Souls.

Instead of soothing her anxieties and fears, the lap, lap, lap filled her with a sense of foreboding.

She moved toward the sound. She paused to listen outside the last door at the end of the hallway.

The lapping wasn't souls in the lake. It was hissing breaths followed by muffled, soft choking sounds coming from within.

She pushed through the surface of the door and into a lighted room.

The overhead fluorescent tubes were dimmer than the hospital rooms she had been visiting lately, but the room was still full of hospital equipment. A maternity ward incubator stood in the center of the room, which had once been, or had been intended to be, a nursery. Blue walls covered in mural collages of clouds, rainbows, fields, and flowers surrounded her. Chairs and settees lined the walls—shoved haphazardly back to make way for equipment. A basinet had been slid into a corner, and blankets and boxes of infant diapers had been stacked carelessly in and atop it.

Several machines fed tubes and wires into the incubator.

An IV drip hung over the chrome and plastic box, half tangled in a duck, bunny, and planet mobile. Occasionally, the mobile chimed a tiny note as if struggling to play a tune.

Beyond the incubator and against the wall beside a floor-to-ceiling window masked by dark blinds, a young woman sat in a wing-backed chair. Her head slumped forward, and dark, tight curls hid her face.

The breathing and weak sobs came from her.

With each sob, the curls shook like dark leaves on wind-blown tree branches. A green library lamp stood on a desk beside her, casting additional light on her lap. In her lap, she held an open book.

Littlest Death slipped closer to her and examined the book. It was *The Velveteen Rabbit*, and the woman's tears made dark circles on a page showing a picture of a fire burning blankets and toys.

Quietly, terrified of what she would find and fighting to keep the dark guilt within her from overwhelming her and chasing her from the room, Littlest Death turned to the incubator.

The child within was a girl, but she was so tiny—so frail and empty that Littlest wanted to reach in and carry his soul away to Underworld.

Without thinking, she slipped a hand into the incubator and touched the child on the forehead—the gentle touch of the lift and pull that would relieve the child's suffering and begin the healing for the young mother.

Cold.

No. Not cold.

The absence of warm.

The absence of life within the living flesh.

Littlest Death recoiled from the child's form. She slipped back until she stood thigh-deep in a vacant settee by a rainbow on the blue wall.

This was *the* child.

The stupid dog had been right.

This was the empty vessel she had created—the soulless thing that should have held the girl she had moved into the body of Paul—Paul, who should have grown up to be a sainted teacher of humanity.

The woman's sobbing stopped.

As if she sensed the presence of Littlest Death, she looked up and whispered, "Please?"

It was only one word, but Littlest Death heard all the horror, hope, fear, and love of the woman's life in that word.

Terror and guilt drove Littlest Death from the room in a rush of panic. She moved more quickly than she knew she could—so quickly that her robes billowed behind her and she didn't have to grab them up. She ran blindly along the hallway, through the veil, past the Pooch of Pain, and along the rivulets, creeks, and rivers of silver light.

Revelation by the Lake

When at last she stopped, she found herself near the worn stone on which she had sat so many times over the years. Instead of peace in her place in Underworld, she felt only the whispered pain of the pleading mother. She saw only the agonized grief on the faces of Paul's parents and his brother in the hospital.

Oh, by all the joys of creation, she wanted her bucket back—to go back to carrying the sparks of life from paramecia and fungi. She wished with all her soul that she had never wished for more than that. She would even be glad to once more and always and forever dive into the deeps of the Marianas Trench and gather spark sludge in the cold and dark.

She wanted to be Littlest Death again, to be the smallest and most insignificant of the blank deaths.

The Dog of Darkness pushed a head under her hand.

Startled, she jumped back.

The Puppy of Eternity sat. All three heads faced her. All six eyes accused her.

"I didn't know," she said. "I couldn't know."

The tail thumped on dark stone. Left cocked to one side as if to ask her a question.

"I'll fix it," she said. "I can fix it."

Right cocked in the opposite direction.

"We just need a soul."

Center Head looked at her feet, as if to say, "That's not a very good idea."

She ignored the heads and moved to the edge of the Lake of All Souls. Just one soul from so many. Billions and billions, maybe trillions and trillions, filled the lake. Just one. All she needed was one, and she could fix what she had done.

She gathered up her hem, knelt on bony knees, and cupped hands into the lake.

Silvery souls shimmered in her hands and flowed between her bony fingers and back into the lake.

She tried again, but she could not hold the liquid life of the Lake of All Souls in her hands. Once a soul returned to the lake, it could no more come back onto the shore than she could create life.

Long and dark was the time she spent kneeling, head bowed like the woman with the book in her lap. Had she eyes with which to cry, she would have poured an eternity of tears into the lake.

The Puppy of Patience sat beside her, waiting silently for her to find a path for them to follow, a way to set things right.

Eventually, that path came to her. If she could not lift a soul from the lake or the streams, then she had to move closer to the flesh. She needed a soul destined for a short life—or a soul fresh from a short life.

Yes. A soul leaving the flesh after a short life. A soul from a life that couldn't possibly make much of a ripple.

That might work.

She would find and take a soul from the brief life of an already dying child.

The idea was simple.

Too simple. She quickly realized it would resolve nothing. It would just change which lump of flesh was empty.

But if she could find a soul in a place with so many dying children that—

She shook her head. It was too much to think about, but she had to find a path.

She tried again.

She had taken a soul and replaced it, but that left an empty body. She could take a soul and fill that body, but there would be another empty body and more grieving parents somewhere.

There had to be other empty bodies. There had to be. The number of bodies was always growing. Humans worried about that—population growth. More humans were being born than were dying.

Paul had gone somewhere. Even if even births and deaths were equal, if a few souls went where Paul went, there had to be more bodies than souls.

Even if there was only one extra empty body, it would mean—

The problem was that her empty body was one everyone knew wasn't supposed to be empty.

Littlest Death saw a glimmer of hope.

She needed a soul from a place that was too crowded and miserable—a place where nobody would notice if a body was empty or if a soul was taken away before it went to the lake. If she got one quick enough and moved it, Oldest wouldn't—

No. It wasn't right. She knew it couldn't be right.

But she had to do something. She had to, and it was all she could think to do. The child in the incubator was destined to live long and well. It was supposed to be the vessel for the little girl who was now a boy and growing and teaching Paul's parents, Paul's community, and Paul's nation.

Any soul from a short-lived body would want to move to a long-lived body next. That just made sense. The other deaths always told her the cycle was about souls learning. So, more time living meant more learning.

She had carried millions of sparks in her bucket. They didn't travel one at a time. The bucket saved time. Even the special trick she alone had for freezing time to scoop up millions of sparks made it clear saving time was good. It had to be good.

The travels from the lake to the flesh were only travels. She couldn't imagine that souls learned much from travelling.

Stories said that mingling in the lake was about what to choose next. All that love and sharing between flowing souls couldn't mean much, could it? If it did, then why did she have to dump buckets full of sparks into the lake? Paramecia sparks couldn't have much of anything to share with humans. She doubted they could feel love. Most of the learning had to happen in the flesh.

She had overheard someone say that the shortest lives often taught the greatest lessons to the souls around them.

If she took a dying child, she'd be helping other souls learn—parents and stuff. If she put it in a better body, she'd be helping the soul she took.

"Right?" she asked the Mutt of Muddle.

Center stared at her in disapproval.

To the Flop-eared Trio, she said, "We have to help."

All three heads flipped back and forth like a herd of fleas had suddenly attacked. Ears flopped. Red eyes rolled.

She ignored the Hound of Hindrance. What could he know?

She had already delivered a soul to another body without bringing it back to the lake. She knew it could be done, and she told herself that this was what Oldest Death meant when he sent her out to set things right.

"I need a place where bodies are being born and dying before souls enter them—a place with empty flesh no soul can, or would, enter."

To prove her enthusiasm for her plan, she leapt up and faced the Hound of Endless Faith. "I can do it! I can fix it!" Once again, she raced off along the shore of the Lake of All Souls. The Dog of Doubt followed, barking its three-toned bark as it ran.

SHANTY TOWN SIDS

In a hovel made of gathered sticks and corrugated tin on a red-dust alley of shanties built of cardboard, tin, and garbage from the city of Dharavi in Mumbai, Littlest Death found the soul she needed.

A gaunt, grimy untouchable father cursed his haggard gap-toothed wife.

Her back to the ranting man and shoulders rolled protectively forward over the silent, day-old infant she held to a flaccid breast, she encouraged the motionless girl to suck.

The man paced and railed, but she kept her back to him, protecting the flickering life at her breast.

The woman uttered prayers in Hindi, but they were not the type of prayers that Littlest Death expected. Littlest, seeing the man screaming at his wife, expected prayers of deliverance from her cruel husband or pleading for the life of her child.

Instead, the woman chanted a quiet prayer to Yama, the oldest and greatest of the Hindi deaths. She prayed for the Atma, the soul, facing choices when leaving the body and moving along in the cycle of living and dying.

Littlest realized that the woman knew her baby was about to leave Overworld.

Tired and terrified, the woman prayed for a best path into the afterlife and into a higher life because the child had been pure and innocent in this life and deserved better in the next.

Littlest Death saw that it was true, and hope rose in Littlest's dark chest because she could make this woman's prayer come true. She would also make the prayer of the woman with the book in her lap come true.

For the first time in her thousand years, she understood that prayers might just work if the bits and pieces of the universe fit together just right, and Littlest was one of those pieces.

In her joy, she thought she now understood what it meant to be a true death.

This was what Oldest Death had wanted her to learn. This, she imagined, was how other deaths found their places and became locked to a metaphor. By serving the prayers of the people of a place and time, they became part of the love that flowed within and lit all souls.

She couldn't help but laugh. It was all so simple.

But, she had to be quick. While she knew she needed to be in this place and time, she also knew she had not been sent for this soul.

Other deaths had snatched souls from her before. St. Francis had, the Wild Hunt, Butterfly. Another death would come for this child.

She could not be seen if she wanted to set things right, raise the soul to a better life, help both women, and move beyond the shame of what she had done.

If she were quick, the other death, the death she did not want to meet, would return to the afterlife without a soul. There would be confusion. There might even be blame.

That would be bad, but it wouldn't be too bad and it might not even happen. She was pretty sure Oldest must have exaggerated his skills. With all the empty bodies and so many souls coming and going in this place, nobody could keep track of who belonged where and in which body.

She moved in close to the child and the praying mother.

The father screamed that the mother had betrayed him, had brought shame to him. He said a girl baby should be put to death, should be burned, should be given to the sacred river alive as an offering to Yama that he might change their fortunes.

The woman protected her child and prayed.

The man calmed a bit and tried to persuade the woman that the child would be better off in the Palace of Yama. There, she could serve and live well and in splendor.

For a moment, the man became silent. While he caught his breath, the woman barely breathed, but she used what breath she had to pray.

Littlest Death wondered that in a place so full of poverty and people the only sounds were the sounds of distant barking, the screaming of another man not far away, and the low quiet chant of the tearless mother.

Littlest reached out and touched the shoulder of the mother to reassure her that her child's soul would live on and live better.

The woman stopped praying. She looked up and straight into Littlest's face. For a long moment, the woman was silent. It was almost as if the mother and the child could both see Littlest.

Perhaps they were both so close to their ends that they could.

The mother nodded and held her child up as if Littlest Death should take if from her.

Littlest Death touched the child, took the tiny hand of the soul within, and lifted her from the flesh.

The woman pulled the flesh back and clasped the lifeless body to her breast again. Carrying her lost child, she walked away from her husband and the darkness of their hovel.

Littlest Death followed her. Outside, they moved in opposite directions along the alleys and trails between tin walls. The mother moved downslope toward the river.

Littlest Death carried the child's soul along a parched, red dust road toward the place where the veil would open for them and let them pass through into Underworld.

As they approached that thin and shimmering gateway between the worlds, a boy appeared. His dark, golden skin and thick black hair glistened as if he had just been oiled after a bath. The golden necklaces and bracelets he wore tinkled like tiny bells, and he smiled in greeting as he walked barefoot toward them.

This meta had to be the death who was supposed to take this child.

Too late, Littlest told herself. *Too late.*

She couldn't duck into a shadow or hide behind a hovel. The child in her arms couldn't be hidden from a death.

This meta would know his own even through walls of Overworld. More important, he would not see Littlest Death's actions as helping the soul.

Certainly, Oldest Death would hear about this.

She couldn't slip the child out of Overworld now that the child's true death had come. A meta appearing was no surprise given the prayers of the child's mother and the outcast status of the family. Even Littlest Death had long ago noticed that the more desperate and terrified humans became, the more certain they were of the form of the soul, the messengers of death, and the nature of the afterlife.

Of course, none of the religions of Overworld had ever gotten the forms right. However, most of them had understood the foundational nature of life, death, and soul.

She gently set the child down. The infant soul stood beside her, tiny hand grasping the smallest bony finger of her hand. Littlest Death did her best to stand straight and show confidence while walking toward the newcomer, but empty shame chilled her chest and neck. She hoped the other death could not see it in her.

The newly arrived meta, a Hindi child of perhaps twelve himself, politely said, "Good, kind Littlest Death, for I know your name and works by the kindness of my teacher, Yama, I offer you greetings and a wish of favor and freedom from the burden of Atma."

Littlest knew the ritual greeting had a correct response, but buckets full of bacteria and fungi didn't require her to know poetic Hindu rituals for death meeting death.

"Hello," she said. "I don't think we've met."

"May it please you, guardian of the first sparks of life who will one day rise to touch and become the heart of Brahma, my legend names me Natchiketa, and I am come to guide this innocent upon the journey into the cycles of life and learning."

Refusing would only make things worse, so she said, "Okay," and urged the tiny soul toward Natchiketa.

The newly dead child looked to Littlest Death, confusion apparent in the wrinkle of her glowing brow.

Littlest Death nodded to reassure her. "Go on," she said. "He'll help you."

The soul moved toward Natchiketa. When they were close, the meta pressed his hands flat together, touched his fingertips to his forehead, then bowed deeply.

The infant soul returned the gesture. She glowed a little brighter and grew a little taller after her bow.

Well, Littlest told herself, maybe it wasn't quite what she had hoped, but it was as it was supposed to be. She'd find another soul. She'd be quicker next time.

Natchiketa crossed his ankles and lowered himself gracefully to a cross-legged seat upon the dusty earth.

The infant, who now seemed closer to five years old than five hours, flawlessly performed the same maneuver.

The two Hindi spirits faced one another, one newly from life and the other, who knew how long, a death. Natchiketa looked up at Littlest Death expectantly.

"I'll just be going," she offered. "Other souls to guard. First sparks to gather, and all. You know." She tried to sidestep around the two.

Natchiketa said, "Sit with us, Littlest Death, who has labored so long upon the Earth in timeless service to the endlessness of life being born into flesh and form. Sit with us and listen as we talk of Atma. Bear witness to this soul's choices and how she recreates herself."

For less than a human heartbeat, Littlest considered running. But, if Natchiketa weren't already going to talk about her, running would certainly cause him to discuss her with Oldest Death.

She decided the least remarkable thing she could do was sit. So far, she was a kind of hero in Natchiketa's eyes. At least, she hoped she was. She had shown up and freed the soul. She had reassured it. She had walked it toward its meeting with its assigned death.

Yeah. That's all she had done. She'd helped him out a little.

Natchiketa couldn't know what she had planned to do.

She crossed her own legs and tried to mimic the graceful, twisting sitting move she'd seen. Her robes tangled. Her legs bent wrong. She fell to her rear in the dust.

When the dust settled, her legs were crossed, sort of, under her robes. She folded her hands in her lap and waited.

Natchiketa nodded. His wide, dark eyes looked into her as deeply as Oldest Death. However, Natchiketa's gaze sent warm, loving kindness spreading through her as if he were pouring it into her.

The Hindu student of Yama said to the new soul, "Here, you step from flesh into spirit, and you may step again into flesh. From the life you left, short though it was, knowing has come to you of that which will help you choose the path you will now walk." He tapped one golden finger against the girl's forehead.

The child nodded, closed her bright, wide eyes, and bowed her head low until her chin rested on her chest. Silently, the child began to glow more brightly.

Natchiketa nodded and smiled. To Littlest Death, he said, "She walks the memories of the life of flesh she has left."

More curious than was probably good for her under the circumstances, Littlest asked, "Do all the souls you gather have to do this?"

The Hindu death child's laugh felt warm and kind. It wasn't like the chilling laughs of Ammit or Baast. It wasn't like the chuckling of the blank deaths who made fun of her for carrying the bucket that let her do her job.

He said, "Kind and glorious carrier of sparks, hear these words and know that I know that you have known their truth even before I spoke them. No soul *must* do this thing or that thing. All souls *must* do everything. This soul chooses to hear my heart in my words. She chooses to pause upon the threshold between Overworld and Underworld. She chooses to remember and to choose. That is all."

Littlest Death watched the recently released soul. The silver-blue glow grew brighter and brighter. The young shade grew again, and now she seemed to be perhaps seven or eight. When the girl had become almost as bright as the boy who walked across the Lake of All Souls, Littlest asked, "Will she move on? Transcend?"

"Yes," Natchiketa said. "As do all."

Littlest Death's chuckle wasn't as kind as Natchiketa's had been. She knew how rare transcendence had to be.

"You find truth funny, Spark Carrier?"

"No. No." Littlest Death composed herself. "Not at all."

Natchiketa tilted his head to the side and appraised her. His earrings tinkled. "I say this—that all souls will move beyond Overworld, Underworld, and our knowing. Do you doubt it?"

She didn't want to argue. She also didn't want Natchiketa to think poorly of her. In fact, she didn't want him to think of her at all, so she held back her nervous, contemptuous laughter. Besides, she wanted to see what came of the child's glowing reverie. That, and getting back to Underworld to figure out what she was going to do next, were more important than the meta's human-imposed beliefs. "No," she managed. "Not at all."

Natchiketa tilted his head to the other side. He tinkled. His dark hair dusted his golden-skinned shoulder. His great, brown eyes asked silent questions.

They sat like that for a while, staring at one another while the child glowed and travelled some internal landscape of life memories.

Finally, Littlest Death couldn't stand the searching, staring questions in his eyes. She tried to avoid his gaze, but she could feel him silently asking her, willing her to explain, to answer the question he had not asked.

The child showed no sign of dimming, and leaving before Natchiketa seemed both rude and ill-advised.

She gave up her silence. "Rumors," she said, "and legends say that one death knew another who once saw a soul walk across the Lake of All Souls."

He nodded. He twisted a wrist and turned his palm up like he held a cup. A bell on his bracelet tinkled. "So it is said."

"There," she said, "in the center of the lake, a single branch that ends in the shape of a hand rose from the lake. In the hand rested the chalice from which all souls flow."

He made the same palm up gesture with his other hand. "The sacred river of all lives."

"The soul rose upward and, in a glorious moment of joy and brilliant light, expanded into the beyond of all we know."

Natchiketa nodded. He pressed his palms together and touched the tips of his fingers to his forehead. "Returned to Brahma." He placed both hands back in his lap. Solemnly, he asked, "This is a thing of humor?"

A little creeped out by how his gestures seemed choreographed to her words, she paused for a moment before she calmed enough to say, "So it happens? You've seen it?" She barely caught herself before adding a "too."

"You doubt such a beautiful thing?"

"No. I mean, yes. I mean … It's just that not one death I have talked to in a thousand years has ever actually seen it happen, so how can you say that all souls eventually do it?"

Natchiketa smiled. "Has one soul done it?" Again, the palm up hand.

She couldn't very well say no. "Legends say so." An uncomfortable certainty grew inside her that his bright, dark eyes saw her deceits.

He nodded slightly. The other palm came up.

She believed in that moment that he knew everything about her and what she was doing—what she had done.

He said, "If one soul has returned to Brahma, all souls can return to Brahma."

"I'm sorry," she said. "I know you've probably been meta for a long time, but I think you and I both know better."

Quietly, gently, he said, "*You* know better. I know nothing at all." He pressed his palms together.

"You know what I mean."

He grinned, touched his forehead, and made a tiny, endearing nod.

His infectious smile made her want to grin, too. It was like an angel smile. It even made her want to laugh with joy, but she couldn't say why. She held it back and said, "I have carried millions of buckets of millions of souls out of Overworld and to the shores of the lake."

"Yes," he said. "You have done this kindness for even the smallest of lives for a thousand years."

"I have poured millions upon millions of souls into the lake."

Again, his grin and tiny nod.

The grin was starting to annoy her. She wondered if he would still smile like that if she sicked the Triple Biter on him. "In fact," she went on, "I have probably brought more souls to the lake than any other death."

"Probably." He turned his serene smile to his glowing charge.

She continued. "I've never seen anything like the legends, so it just can't be true that all souls transcend if not even one of those millions and millions has."

"*Truth*?" Bracelets tinkled.

His gaze, fixed on the glowing child, did not keep her from knowing the single word was meant for her. Hot shame washed through her. She was trying to lie to herself by lying to Natchiketa. She knew it and knew he knew she knew.

A cold wave of anger washed away her shame. She gathered herself to rise and tell this grinning meta child death that he had no business looking down at her. Her millions upon millions of souls meant something. He owed her some respect. It was just luck that he hadn't been given the bucket job.

Luckily, the glowing infant chose that moment to dim a bit, lift her head, and open her eyes.

Natchiketa apparently lost all interest in Littlest Death. "And?" Natchiketa asked the child.

The infant managed to grin the very same serene, stupid grin as Natchiketa. She said, "The first boon you wished of Yama was peace and prosperity for the father who sold you to Death."

Natchiketa nodded and stood.

The girl stood.

Littlest Death had a little trouble untangling her legs and robes, so by the time she was up the child and the meta death had walked along the dusty street toward the shadow where the veil would part.

"What?" she called after them. "What's she going to do?"

Natchiketa paused and turned, but the girl walked on and slipped away into Underworld on her own.

"Well?" Littlest asked.

"She chooses to return to the flesh in the hopes of creating peace for her father."

"The father who cursed her? Who wanted to kill her?"

Natchiketa nodded, smiled, placed his hands flat together, and bowed.

"How?" Littlest asked.

When Natchiketa stood, he began to slip through the veil, fading away until only his brilliant grin remained. That grin spoke and then was gone. "One soul's love," it said.

Littlest stood alone on the dusty street of one of the worst places in all the Overworld. Here, she had come before, stopped time, and gathered bucket after bucket of horrid, tiny sparks—sparks that in flesh had killed cattle, dogs, cats, and millions of people.

Now, she stood surrounded by the place's stench and chaos for a long moment.

Around her, dogs barked, children cried, and parents screamed their anger and fear at one another and the world.

In the distance, a loud, hungry newborn cried out.

Beyond that, woven in and out of the cries of fear and pain, a young woman sang a high song of joy for the dawning of a new day.

Not far from Littlest Death, and near where Natchiketa had disappeared, an ancient woman stepped from the cavernous shadows of her hovel entrance. Into the baked, red dust she carefully poured water from a weak soup she had made the day before.

As the soup poured out onto the earth, she murmured a prayer that the tiny lives in the soil would accept her abundance and thrive.

Not knowing why, Littlest Death began to shake uncontrollably.

To stop the shaking, she ran.

She ran from the confusion and pain of such a terrible place, and she ran toward the order and darkness of Underworld where all rivers of light and life flow outward from a center she understood less and less with each trip she made into Overworld.

Self-flagellation

Finding her way back to the dark, restored Victorian where the young woman read children's stories to empty flesh was not nearly as difficult as finding the house the first time. Once, she took a wrong branching, but the Canine of Correction seemed to know what she was about. Right and Center grabbed her robes while Left strained back over its shoulder to point the correct way.

"Thanks." She moved quickly along the last rivulet, through the veil, and up to the only lighted room in the house.

The home wasn't like the shanty town where nobody had currency and families might trade a girl child for gold or even for bread and rice.

As she slid along corridors, up the stairs, and past closed doors, she wondered how this woman had come to live in such a huge, empty house. Clearly, she had accumulated a horde of the tokenized fantasy humans traded for energy, food, shelter, and objects.

Currency.

Littlest took small pride in having remembered the idea's name.

She thought about the family she'd seen at the hospital. Even though she had listened to a thousand stories about humans and spent a thousand years carrying sparks from Overworld to Underworld, she had only seen a few families—most from a distance. The family outside the hospital room where her mistakes began all seemed close in their grief and fear.

This woman was alone. Littlest was pretty sure there was usually a man. That family had been made up of a woman, a man, and another child. The family in India had a man—even if he wasn't very nice. She was pretty sure once humans needed male and female bodies to make new soul vessels. Littlest remembered some scary stories about how human men and women made babies. She didn't like the stories, but other deaths seemed to find them very funny.

Sure, she'd heard that wasn't the only way in 21st Century United Sates. She also knew that men like the one in the hovel were probably not much help with a baby, but humans did seem to grow families to fit the space available, and this house was really big.

In the lighted room, the incubator hadn't moved. The tiny flesh husk within still pulsed and breathed. The woman still sat in the chair—

No. *She* didn't.

It was a different woman—a taller woman, but about the same age. She wore darker, more formal clothing. Littlest Death thought maybe the dark clothes were business clothes—or, maybe, they were for a funeral or some other metaphored ritual.

Littlest chastised herself for not paying better attention to the stories about humans in 21st Century United States. Once she had been assigned, she should have asked some questions. She should have spent some time in Overworld observing, but she'd been too excited. Then, she'd been too busy trying to make things right.

The new woman's face was harder, more rigid than the earlier, crying woman, but the book on her lap suggested she, too, had been reading to the soulless flesh.

Littlest Death slipped over near her and saw that *The Velveteen Rabbit* had been replaced by a book called *My Two Mommies.*

This woman's dry eyes shone red in the weak, pale light from overhead fluorescents. Mascara smeared her cheek, and she stared at the incubator as if staring might somehow change the plastic and chrome crèche into a hand-crafted, wooden rocking crib that matched the Victorian décor of the rest of the house.

Well, if things had worked out the way Littlest Death had planned, everything would have been fine. This woman and the other woman could have believed all they wanted that prayers and staring had magical powers.

Of course, Littlest's plan hadn't worked.

She wished it had. She had even dared to hope that Oldest Death would have seen how hard she had worked to fix things and maybe—just maybe—wouldn't send her to Antarctica to gather sparks from pink algae snow.

She hated the cold, hard tightening in her chest. She hated herself and what she had done—and what she had failed to do. She had created suffering for the people outside the hospital room. She had caused terrible pain for these two women. The tiny bit of trust she had developed with Oldest Death was gone, and the other deaths would laugh at her harder than ever.

She deserved it.

That's how it should be, she told herself. She should be laughed at. Not a million, million tiny sparks could have prepared her for one, single human soul.

She was Littlest Death because she was only fit to gather the littlest souls.

The sad woman stared.

The empty husk lay still.

The incubator hummed quietly, moving air in and out and warming the empty body within.

Littlest Death couldn't help—couldn't fix this.

She pulled up her cowl, gathered her robes, and trudged back to Underworld to report her failure to Oldest Death. He would be unimpressed.

Not Quite the Word

Unimpressed wasn't quite the word.

Slow and reluctant, she made the long trip back along the labyrinthine rivulets and rivers of flowing souls. She still had the Puppy of Heel Tripping at her back, but the closer she got to Oldest Death, the more reluctant she became to tell Oldest what she had and had not done.

He had believed in her—believed she could and would fix her mistake.

She had tried. Hadn't she tried? Yes. Certainly, she had tried.

She arrived at the arena to find it full. Once again, she was late for an assignment session. At least her luck was consistent.

Entering the full arena felt like moving in the darkness of the Marianas against a cold, living current. In spite of her hopes that no other death would notice her, she scanned the circles of seats for some supporting gaze.

Baast, at least, nodded to her. Azrael glanced her way. Ereshkigal's normal seat was empty. She was probably off on a human soul retrieval or some other important task.

She thought she saw Natchiketa's grin nested in the black mass of robes and dark cowls on the far side of the arena. The rest of the many deaths did as she hoped and ignored her like they always did, but now it hurt more than it ever had.

Oldest Death on his dais showed no sign of noticing her. He droned on about the ancient trust and duty of all deaths.

She dejectedly climbed the tiers and took her place. As she settled into her seat, for just a moment she felt a little joy. In a way, failure had let her fall back into the familiar role of being invisible and unimportant.

The women with the empty child hadn't been expected. They were in so much pain because of what Littlest Death had done. They were, in some ways, much worse off than the family she had seen at the hospital. At least that family had a body named Paul and had moved on toward their healing.

A few of Oldest Death's droning words came to her like an echo on mountain winds, "… and everything living dies …"

He was right. *Everything* died.

Every member of every family, each and every one, would die just like the child had died. The soul might be eternal. It might come back to the lake, return to the flesh, and come back to the lake forever.

Natchiketa didn't think so. Not forever.

Might.

Paul had gone on to some other place or some other cycle.

Might.

Who knew what happened to a soul once the tree of life lifted the chalice and the transcendent soul disappeared?

She didn't, and she was one of a handful of deaths who had actually seen it happen.

So, just when and why had she started thinking in terms of her causing good deaths or bad deaths? She had never suffered from such doubts while wielding her bucket.

In the larger universe that held both Underworld and Overworld, was a birth more important—happier—than a death? She knew from experience that a death was just a tiny interruption in perceptions that resulted in a new beginning for the soul.

Atma. That's what Natchiketa had called the soul. The Atma rode the flesh for a time then left it.

From the perspective of the melding of spirits in the Lake of All Souls, life and death were exactly the same.

At least, life and death had always been the same before. Other fungi didn't cry if a fungus died in the woods. Nobody lamented the loss or the birth of a paramecium—not even other paramecia.

Okay, platypuses seemed to care about one another, but it wasn't the same kind of caring the humans seemed to bring to birth and death.

She caught herself thinking in terms of making people—fleshed-in souls—happy or sad.

Ridiculous. A soul was a soul whether in the flesh or out.

In the center of the arena, Oldest Death had started giving out assignments. She barely heard him.

While she pondered this new idea of caring about endings that are beginnings and the same for all living things, the arena emptied one death at a time.

It wasn't until Oldest Death stood right in front of her, his dark robes wrinkled and waving near her feet that she looked up, startled, and realized she sat alone with him in the arena.

"I'm surprised to see you," he said.

This took her back. He was never surprised. A being born in the first breath of the universe couldn't be surprised. At least, she didn't think he could. Her recent experiences made her wonder if what she thought she knew was actually an illusion of certainty she had created while dealing with millions of sparks and convincing herself of her own importance.

Oldest Death had been there when infinite potential had collapsed into finite reality. He had been part of the before, and he was part of both Overworld and Underworld because he had existed before both.

She had overheard some deaths claim that Underworld only existed because he was in it. If he should ever ascend, they said, Underworld would pop out of existence like a child's soap bubble blown at the snout of a dog.

His long silence made her uncomfortable. She said, "I had a plan."

"Yes?"

"It didn't work."

"I see." Being faceless didn't stop him from peering into her deepest doubts and bringing them to light.

"The child's body still has no soul."

"And?"

"The empty baby is the child of two mothers," she said, as if it might mean something important to an eternal creature.

Oldest Death said nothing.

"They were very happy until I stole the soul of their baby." She tried once more to tell herself that happy and sad meant nothing when dealing with the larger context of life and death.

She couldn't believe herself. She had seen too much.

Oldest Death said, "Your assignment?"

She looked at the hem of her robe where it covered her feet and shook her head. After a few moments of his dark silence, she looked up to see how angry he was.

Oldest Death's hood tilted to one side like Center Head on the Puppy of Doubt.

"One soul ascended one life too early," she added. "The wrong soul went to the emptied shell. The empty body has no soul."

"So, you haven't finished."

Confused, she searched the eternal emptiness inside his cowl. Of course, his shadowed eye sockets gave her no hint about what he was thinking. She said, "I tried to steal a soul before it went to the lake."

He loomed.

"I failed," she said.

"Hmm." He bent close to her and whispered, "You are certain?" Then, he stood straight, turned away, walked down the tiers and out of the arena.

She sat on her cold stone seat alone with her doubts and fears.

She was sure.

Well, she had been sure.

She had been full of her own failure. He should have punished her. At the very least, he should have sent her back to Overworld with her bucket.

Doubt and frustration battled in her tiny, bony body. They became swirling, cold fire, rising up and pushing at her throat, begging to become a scream. In a very unearthly fashion, she checked to be sure she was alone in the arena—*really alone.*

She was.

Her death scream roared upward, bounced off the cavernous roof, echoed from every curved tier of stone seats, reverberated, and finally lapped gently at the stones at her feet.

She was not certain.

Her certainty had always been a lie. It was a lie when she counted the sparks in her bucket. It was a lie when she told herself the boy was ready to be taken. It was a lie when she sat with Natchiketa and his shining charge.

It was a lie now.

How many lies had she told herself? Had she ever truly believed them? The certainty had been a way of convincing herself she didn't need to believe inconvenient truths.

She was certain she was important because she carried millions of souls, but she wanted all along to carry humans. She was certain that Oldest Death and all the others would accept her as one of them if she retrieved human souls. She had also told herself that she had failed and all the deaths would reject her because she was not like them.

Even so, the few she counted as kind to her had smiled and nodded as she entered the arena in shame.

The certainty of rejection because of her shame and failure was as much a lie as the certainty of acceptance because of her success.

Now, alone with the truth, she was still Littlest Death—still the death of small things because she couldn't be trusted with larger souls.

No. That was self-pity—another lie.

Oldest Death still trusted her. He had not sent her back to the bucket and sludge in the Marianas Deeps. She was not on her way to Antarctica to look for pink snow.

Confused and afraid of herself and her own thoughts, she trudged out of the arena and along the worn paths toward the Lake of All Souls.

The Dog of Dejection met her at the arena entrance.

Center Head looked up sadly while Left and Right slavered and slobbered and took over the body in a dance that said, *We like you. We'll always like you. Come play with us.*

Ripples and Puzzles

Not even tossing stones into the placid, blue-silver surface of the Lake of All Souls calmed her.

All three heads of the Dog of Disgust followed her bony hand every time she lifted a stone. All three heads dropped a little in disappointment every time she tossed the stone into the lake instead of onto the shadowy terrain surrounding them.

Still, each time she lifted a new stone, the heads came up, the red eyes burned brighter, and the tongues lolled.

A part of her knew she was torturing the Hound of Hopelessness.

A part of her told herself it was okay because that's how Oldest Death and the other deaths treated her.

The rest of her knew better. No matter how hard she tried to be certain they hated her, she couldn't completely believe it.

She was like the Dog with Three Brains: feeling, doubting, and sure.

No.

Left, Right, and Center were smarter. They all knew who they were and what they had to do. Their job was to play and grow up into a very scary guardian of paths from Overworld into Underworld.

What was her job?

A voice broke through her veil of self-pity and victim rage. "Abusing yourself?"

She spun to see who had managed to sneak up on her and the Puppy of Prescience, who always knew when someone was coming.

Ereshkigal, of course. One of the older deaths and winged in the bargain, she knew the ways of sneaking.

The Sumerian meta settled down on her hawk's legs under her normal golden robes, but Ereshkigal did not sit completely, as if she disliked touching her rear to the stones or might need to leap up quickly and fly away.

"I come here to be alone." Littlest Death threw another stone.

The Canine of Contention growled at Ereshkigal.

Unimpressed, Ereshkigal picked up a pebble so small that it barely covered the first digit of her finger. She said, "You are never alone," then she casually tossed the pebble over her shoulder.

All three heads snapped back in the direction of the pebble's flight. The Daft Darkness Dog bolted off into the shadows.

“Now you are alone with me,” Ereshkigal said, “and you are still not alone.”

“Did Oldest send you?”

“He is very busy in the Middle East again.”

“None of your Sumerians are dying there?”

“Dying. Died. Will have died. Had died. Has died. Will die. Thousands upon thousands. All is as it should be. I will be there again soon enough.”

Littlest Death didn’t know what to say to that. Something terrible was happening again, she guessed. If thousands were dying, or would die, or whatever, then thousands of families were grieving.

No. She couldn’t think about that. It was far away, and it had nothing to do with her.

They sat in silence, staring at the lake. Tiny ripples lapped at her feet. The glow surrounded them.

The Dog of Deliverance returned. All three heads dropped a pebble at Ereshkigal’s feet. Apparently, hawk goddess or not, Ereshkigal was now a very good friend.

Ereshkigal selected an offering and tossed again.

The Dash Hound was gone.

Three more times, the Dog of Duplication returned and ran back into the shadows for a stone. Each time she tossed one, three returned. The little pile of pebbles at Ereshkigal’s feet grew.

Littlest did her best to ignore the goddess and dog playing beside her.

Finally, Ereshkigal said, "A riddle, then, and I will leave you to be not alone in peace."

"I'm not Sumerian."

"You, Littlest Death, are a pebble." Ereshkigal swept up the dog's pile of pebbles and tossed them all far out into the lake. They spread out in a great arc, and each fell separately to the silver surface. Ripples spread out from each. A chaos of ripples spread, each tangling with those of the next stone. Soon, the surface was a rippling, undulating mess. Where ripples collided, some cancelled one another, others seemed to join together and grow into larger ripples. Full circle ripples, short curved waves, and odd diamond patterns all spread outward from the center where they had begun.

Annoyed by the chaos, Littlest turned to Ereshkigal, but the meta was gone.

Tiny, intermittent slaps licked at the shore at her feet as different fragments of ripples came to shore.

The Dog of Devotion sat once more at her side. All three heads dropped pebbles then peered at her through worried, burning eyes.

"That's not a riddle," Littlest said.

Center barked once.

"Well," she added, "it's a stupid riddle."

They sat in silence for a while, Littlest mesmerized by the slowly smoothing surface, and all three Doting Dog heads mesmerized by Littlest Death.

Finally, as if staring blankly at the interlacing patterns had caused the universe to place the idea in her mind, she whispered, "I understand."

Center cocked. Left whimpered. Right nosed a pebble closer to her foot.

She stood. "It's why there are so many deaths in the arena," she said. "It's so obvious."

The Hound of Hubris whimpered in his weird, three-toned voice.

"Oldest Death can't keep up. He can't possibly be there for every death in every life. He just can't, so he needs us."

"No," she said. "That's not quite right. He made us. He split us off from himself because he needed us."

She laughed out loud, grabbed her bucket, and jumped up. "It's getting worse," she said. "There are more bodies than souls."

Center shook his head. The triple bark echoed in the halls of Underworld.

Excited, Littlest went on. "Taking one soul from a place of many deaths wasn't enough. I need to go to terrible places where there aren't enough deaths doing the work. I need chaos. I need to move lots and lots of souls!"

A three-toned yip only made her more excited to start.

"That's it! I'll move lots, and I only have to keep one extra soul."

All three heads cocked left. Six ears flopped. Six burning eyes seemed to say they doubted her plan.

"No. It's okay. The ripples of all the shuffled souls will still touch, right? It'll be like being in the lake if there's lots. Each moved soul will have others who are the same."

Left chuffed. Right yipped. Center shook his head so hard his ears slapped Left and Right.

"Really," she said, and she was off again.

The Big Shuffle

She ran, the Heel Hound chasing and nipping at her flying robes. She ran to make herself known, to be understood, to be what no death believed she could be. She ran to make right that which she had made wrong.

Chaos in the Middle East meant a thousand, thousand ripples intersecting. Azrael would be there serving all three religions. Oldest Death would be there gathering in the thousands. Blanks and other metas would be there—even Ereshkigal would be there. Not even the most experienced deaths would be able to keep track of all the death.

That's where she would find the first soul she needed, and she did.

A thin brown man stood over him. Covered in white dust from shattered buildings, tears streaking his cheeks, the man prayed to the three-faced patriarchal god. The infant in the rubble barely breathed, but his remaining eye still watched his father, still pleaded to be helped, saved from the pain of what had happened.

Littlest Death knew the father would grieve. She knew the child would be freed of pain. She knew Oldest Death or one of the metas would come if she didn't hurry. If Oldest became aware that she had taken this first soul, he would know she took all the souls she planned to take. She had to be quick.

One tiny, bloody hand stuck out from the rubble.

The father made the sign of the cross and held the crux amulet he wore around his neck to the child's lips.

The infant was too young to understand.

Littlest Death lifted the child's soul, and they walked away and through the veil.

Buddha Child

She placed the soul in a birthing body in Bangladesh where the soul had not yet arrived. She took some pride in the reaction of the kind mother and father who bawled and hugged one another as the nearly lifeless body of their baby took deeper and deeper breaths until it opened its eyes and began to cry. At the very moment the veil parted, she took up the tiny spark that should have joined that child's flesh.

She placed it in her bucket for later—her one extra soul.

Not far from that place, she visited an infant dying of hunger in a shanty town alley where its mother had been killed.

She gathered up the child without pause and dashed off into Underworld and up along the rivers to a branch that took her back down to another passage and veil. There, she found another newborn and slipped the child into that flesh. She gathered up the new spark as it entered through the veil.

Soul after soul, she lifted, carried, and delivered without ever bringing one to the Lake of All Souls where it might lose form, commune with other souls, learn, grow, and choose a new life.

She took, delivered, and took again.

She lifted old life from flesh and deposited it in new flesh. She used the time power of her bucket to move with the speed of near omnipresence.

What mattered to Littlest Death was scattering enough pebbles on the waters to make it impossible to untangle the ripples. Not even Oldest Death could see so far and so well as to untangle ripples if enough pebbles hit the surface.

And once the ripples were hopelessly tangled, she could place her one extra soul.

She was driven. She was more death than any death had ever been.

And after a time, she found herself in an affluent home at the edge of Dehradun in the Himalayan foothills of Uttarakhand, India.

The saffron-clad Monk beside the unmoving infant told her parents, "No soul has chosen this child."

The father, a man in a white, western shirt and creased slacks stepped forward, fists balled. The mother, a woman wearing a traditional *ghagri* dress, *choli*, and *orni*, jingled as the bells on her wrists moved quickly to restrain the man.

Unperturbed, the Monk touched his hand to the still infant's head. He breathed on the child's face. He raised a bell in his other hand and shook it. The tinkle of the bell filled the room and rang loud in Littlest Death's ears.

She paused in her rush.

The fear and grief of these parents had drawn her. The flesh breathed, but the Monk had said no soul had chosen the body.

Here was the proof that her plan was working. Here was an empty body. Now, she just had to keep going.

The father said to his wife, "Get this superstitious liar out of my house."

"Respect," the wife snapped.

"He shows us none. He'll have no tithe from us."

"For your child," she said. "Respect for your child."

Littlest Death stepped closer. Perhaps the odd tone of the bell drew her in. Perhaps the man's rage or the woman's calm drew her nearer.

Fully stopped in her frenzy of taking and giving, she looked down on the face of the empty little body.

Pinched, dark red, and squinty, it looked more like rotted potatoes she had seen when taking a soul from the garbage dumps near Mombasa than it looked like a human being.

The man said, "This is your child. It is not mine."

The woman slapped him. Her bells tinkled.

The Monk gently rang his bell again. The sweet tone resonated with the sound of the bracelets.

"Stop that!" The man lunged for the Monk's bell.

The Monk was quick for his age, and he was old—very old. Something about him reminded Littlest of Oldest Death. She imagined it was that feeling he had seen everything that had ever been or ever could be.

The man missed his grab. The lunge threw him off balance and he fell to the rug at Littlest Death's feet.

Peering down at the man, she saw the pattern in the elaborate carpet, a carpet of maroon and gold and blue that drew her attention into an interlocking geometry that interlaced into warp and weft to create greater and greater patterns.

The bell rang a third time.

The man on the floor sobbed.

Littlest Death found herself following the intersections of circles and squares and stars ever inward until she saw the center of the rug—the center of the circles that had seemed to her to be chaos at first.

Almost absently, Littlest Death moved to the child, tipped her bucket, and poured her one extra soul into the flesh.

The Monk smiled at her as if he could see her. "Thank you," he said.

The child gasped. Eyes fluttered. Tiny hands grasped at the air.

The woman let out a tiny squeak, as if she had been hit hard in chest and held no more air than a mouse.

The man still wept on the floor.

Again, the Monk looked straight at Littlest Death and said, "Thank you. I cannot imagine the cost to you."

Confused and unsure how to respond to a monk who seemed to see her, Littlest Death turned away and walked slowly through the veil and into Underworld.

There, she found her friend, the Three Faces of Faithfulness. She sat beside him. Her bucket was empty. She held no child soul's hand. Her plan to confuse all the deaths and find one extra soul to take to the women in the Victorian had been ended by flesh never meant to live and the bell of a monk.

There were no extra souls. There was only extra flesh waiting for a spark of spirit—for some glowing heart to grow and flow from the lake. Perhaps the soul that came to an empty child didn't need to be a child's soul. Perhaps it could have been a platypus, a lizard, or a rat the last time it had worn flesh.

Who was she to think she understood the journey of heart each soul, no matter how small, took before walking the Earth in the form of a human child?

She buried her face in fur, and, for the first time since she became self-aware, she wept.

Confession

She named the ice in her chest Shame. It was a thing she had not understood. It was one of many things she had not understood. With the Dog of Darkness at her heels, she searched out Oldest Death where he gathered in the legions of souls for which he was responsible. She found him in a field of poppies at the edge of the veil between Underworld and Overworld.

Just beyond the veil, shadowed in his robes and cowl, he ushered through ten columns of souls—an army marching in step and streaming inward and upward, marching alongside the rivulets, streams, and rivers of flowing spirit. Most were men, but among them she saw the innocent mothers, fathers, sons, and daughters that the dimmest human souls called collaterals.

Few of them carried the relief she had seen on the faces of the infants she had freed from pain and fear.

Instead, most carried themselves as she did—burdened by shame and the weight of failure. She could have stepped in among them, matched their step, and marched upstream to the Lake of All Souls. There, she wondered if she might be able to step into the glow of mingling souls and disappear forever.

But it was a foolish thought, and she was not a human soul come to Underworld from some pointless catastrophe of pride and greed. She was a death, and she had failed in her assignment again.

Worse, she had made her own mistake into more mistakes out of deceitful pride and desire. If certainty had been a lie, deceit in the name of hope was a self-induced wound.

Once, she had believed herself better than other deaths, but she had proven herself less. Once, she believed herself more than the humans she hoped to help, but she had proven the ambition, pride, and arrogance in her heart was worse than theirs.

Approaching Oldest Death, she believed that she belonged in the ranks of the trudging, shamefaced dead under his careful watch.

He saw her. She felt his gaze, but he did not speak to her.

To avoid the moment when he would, she bent and pulled a tiny spark from a trampled and broken yellow flower. She dropped the spark in her empty bucket.

The souls streamed past, and she followed them through the veil. There, she backed into a niche in the stone wall and waited. The Dog of Death found her and sat beside her while she searched for the words she must say.

When the ranks of the dead had passed, Oldest Death gestured to her to fall in with him and follow them upstream toward the lake.

For some time, they walked in the perfect dead silence of Underworld.

Finally, she said, "I failed."

"How?"

"I thought I could make it *appear* as though I had set things right. I thought that if it looked right, it would be right. I tried to—" her voice caught.

"Look at these many souls, Littlest Death."

She looked upstream and along the ranks of marching dead and took that moment to gather her wits.

Oldest Death said, "I have no time for your pride."

"Yes," she said, and her shame hurt as if she were flesh. It stabbed at her and tore at her chest. "I'm sorry."

"One body that should carry a soul is empty of soul."

"Yes."

"And that cannot be overlooked." His voice was flat. He neither accused her nor confirmed that he forgave.

"I thought you—"

"You thought you understood me."

She nodded. "I thought you made us."

"I did."

She stopped moving.

He walked on a few paces then turned back to face her.

She stood in silence trying to figure out what he thought—what he meant—but the pain of shame in her chest was too great. Oldest Death wasn't a mystery she could understand. At last, she said, "The empty child is my fault." She shook her head. "I told myself it must have happened before. I told myself it didn't matter in the large scale of things."

"Each death is the most important death ever," he said.

She nodded. "And each birth."

The souls silently marched away into the caverns of the dead.

Oldest Death gestured at the disappearing throng. "All of these know they will learn and live again. They will choose new lives and growth."

She nodded.

"How many souls did you steal that choice from?"

"I did not count."

"Twelve hundred and seven," he said.

She clutched at the pain in her chest. He had not been fooled at all. He had seen it all, known it all. He had— "You let me do it?"

"Like them, you decide who you wish to be," he said. "You create your burdens. I am only Oldest Death. Who am I to stop you from choosing?"

"But you let me—"

For a glaring, icy moment, he gave her his undivided attention.

She froze.

He said, “Go. Decide who and what you are.”

Oldest Death followed the army of the dead upstream to the lake, where each and every one would enter the lake, would commune with so many others, would be freed from their regrets and pain, would be overcome by love and brought to the shores of the lives they would choose next—the lives in which they would learn what they needed to bring them one day to the moment when each would walk across the lake’s surface, reach the center of all things, stand beside the branch of the tree, and touch the chalice.

Natchiketa had been right. If one soul transcended, all souls transcended.

Each and every soul Oldest Death returned to the lake, no matter how much shame and guilt and fear they carried, would once more know hope and once more begin anew.

Hope.

Life is hope.

The chalice poured life into the world, and with life came death to give it meaning—Oldest Death first and then the others and even her.

She sat in her darkness and wept for those she had wronged.

The Hound of Hurting sat beside her, somehow managing to push all three heads against her back and shoulder.

Littlest Death Is Littlest Death

If pride and ambition had taken her along the path of failure to her shame, only a path of humility could redeem her.

She walked in the shadows trying to imagine what humility should look like.

One head of the Hound of Honesty barked. She wasn't sure which head, but she knew what it meant. Thinking about how humility *should* look was not a path of humility. It was just another path of pride.

A glow came from the bucket in her hand, and she remembered the tiny spark of life from the broken poppy. It, just as much as each of the marching men and women, needed to return to the lake.

Without thought or decision, she walked the caverns and rivers until she stepped through a veil and into a meadow. There, she tapped her bucket to stop time then moved to a dying colony of bacteria living in the dark and damp beneath a small stone in the sun beside a marsh. She gathered them into her bucket.

Wandering thus and gathering tiny sparks, she passed frozen days, weeks, and years, searching for contentment in who and what she was, for she was nothing except Littlest Death. To wish to be more was to fail at being what she was.

And even in this, she failed.

No matter how hard she tried, no matter how much she sought to feel the spark of every life, to know the importance of every spark, to understand that she was responsible for her tiny piece of the tapestry of intermingling ripples, she could not help but feel she could be more—do more.

And always when she returned to Underworld, the Dog of the Damned followed her.

Every time she looked at it, she remembered what she had done, what she had tried to become, and how stupid she had been.

Each time she sat still, it brought her a pebble or three.

Each time it looked at her expecting her to play as she once had, she resented it more. Each time it yipped or Center cocked his head, or one of its stupid ears flopped over, she felt more and more of an urge to rage against the creature.

When she could no longer stand the sight of the thing, she pelted it with stones and screamed for it to leave her alone.

While it shied away from her, hurt radiating from all six burning eyes, she ran away and hid.

Skipping Stones

Nothing good had come of shuffling souls to cover up her failure—nothing except that while waiting at a home birth for a short-life soul in a mountain town in Colorado, she had watched a group of children behind the house skipping stones across a pond. She had brought that idea back through the veil.

So, she had ceased to sit on her worn rock and had begun, instead, to stand and flip flat stones into the Lake of All Souls.

The Dog of Abandonment had left her alone. That, or he had just not found her.

Perhaps the damned thing couldn't smell her darkness. Perhaps it had come to its senses and stopped looking for her. That was best, she thought. It should find a death worth its time. She would never be a normal death, and the Dog of Dependence would eventually grow up and need to find a river into the world where it could guard against heroes and heroines who thought sneaking into the afterlife was their duty.

Certainly, nobody ever in the history of history had thought it a good idea to sneak into Underworld to save the lost soul of a fungi—or even a platypus. She would be forever useless to the Dog of Deterrence.

At first, she had found very few flat stones, but as she sought after them, she became better at finding them. Practice and time developed her skill to the point that on a good toss, she could get twelve skips and deliver a flat stone far out into the glowing lake.

Now, on a good skip, she would settle back to lean against her thinking stone and watch the twelve concentric ripples interacting. Tiny waves collided and built. A wave encountered a trough and cancelled—both disappearing forever.

She was like that, she thought. Invisible to the deaths. Meaningless to the large souls seeking wisdom and, perhaps, one day transcendence.

Still, she was. She did what she did. At least she had that even though she deserved so much less.

The last ripples of an especially good toss lapsed into silence at her feet. She stared at the place where the silvery, liquid merging of all souls met the black basalt edge of the lake, and she found herself wondering why Underworld was made of black basalt when it could just as easily have been made of anything at all.

"Have you solved my riddle?" Ereshkigal once again stood next to her without warning.

"Yes," she said.

Oldest Death's voice said, "I don't think she has."

Littlest Death jumped up from her stone, twisted in the air, and nearly fell over. Both deaths were there. She hadn't seen Ereshkigal since she had set her the riddle, and she hadn't seen Oldest Death since she had confessed.

Ereshkigal, she was almost happy to see. Oldest Death, though. For him to be here was—

She didn't know what it meant, but it couldn't be good, and his presence made her shame sharper and colder in her chest.

"Watch," Oldest Death said to her.

She stared. She couldn't do anything else.

He gathered up a handful of pebbles and tossed them out into the lake. A hundred pebbles spattered the surface, and a hundred sets of ripples expanded. As always, they tangled and broke and built and died. As always, she watched, though she felt the gazes of both deaths on her.

Ereshkigal said, "What is the answer?"

Littlest Death said, "Every ripple is a life."

Oldest Death said, "Almost."

Littlest Death said, "It is. I know it. You don't have to—"

Oldest Death interrupted her. "Continue to bring the tiny sparks through the veil. Perhaps in another thousand years, you'll understand."

Before she could say anything, he was gone.

Littlest stood with her back to the lake, facing Ereshkigal. The brightness of the lake lit up Ereshkigal's ancient face. Shadows they both cast shifted on the cavern wall.

"I think you know now," Ereshkigal said.

"What?" she demanded.

"Yes," Ereshkigal said. "I think you know the full answer. You were only ever wrong by one soul."

"I did it!" she yelled. "I told everyone I did it! I screwed things up. Why would you come here and remind me? Why are you all so cruel? I did it! I'm the one!"

Ereshkigal nodded and said, "Just so." Then, she, too, turned and strode away.

Alone again, Littlest Death tried to calm herself. She tried to skip a stone, but it went in on edge and sank, leaving only one set of ripples behind.

She tried again, and she failed again.

Falling back onto her worn stone, she let a familiar feeling envelope her. Sitting in her place, it felt right to throw one stone.

One stone. One set of ripples.

The ripples spread outward. One expanding, curved edge moved toward her.

"I'm the one," she said. "I know it," she said. "I messed everything up."

The tiny waves began to lap at the stone at her feet.

"I'm sorry," she said. "I'm the one."

The Hound of Healing appeared next to her. He pressed against her.

She jumped up in surprise. Seeing him enraged her. She wanted to be alone—wanted to be left alone. She grabbed up her bucket and swung it, catching the creature's shoulder just behind Left.

As soon as the bucket hit, she regretted her rage, but it was too late.

The dog, her only friend, staggered sideways and stepped into the silvery shine of the Lake of All Souls.

Right yelped as if in pain. Center looked up at her, quiet hurt in his flame-red eyes. As the Hound of Grief melted into the Lake of All Souls, Left howled long and sad.

She reached out for Left's neck, but he dodged her grasp, protecting her from herself even to his last moment.

Then, he was gone. The cavern was silent. She was alone.

Only his ripples remained, lapping against the shore at her feet.

She fell back on her rock. In shocked silence, she stared for eons or seconds at the place where the Puppy of Perfect Love had melted away and joined the zillion souls.

A deeper, darker emptiness than she had ever known threatened to crush her chest. What had he ever done to her except give endlessly and unconditionally?

She had become nothing. She had become less than Littlest Death—less than even the paramecia sparks she gathered.

To the place where he had been, she said, "Trikéfalo."

The ripples spread outward.

She spoke to the ripples. "I found you a name. Trikéfalo."

His last ripple slapped against the rock at her feet.

"Triké."

The surface stilled.

She stared at a trillion souls and saw none.

Into the silence, she whispered, "You made ripples."

"You were a pebble," she said.

"I'm a pebble," she said.

"Love makes ripples that build."

She took up one last pebble and tossed it in a high arc over the lake. "I'm a pebble," she said, again.

In her mind, she heard Ereshkigal laughing.

The Obvious Lie

The lie was so obvious. It seemed so silly, so foolish. She'd been telling herself the lie since the first moment she realized she was. She had thought she was alone. She had always thought she was alone—separate from the other deaths, from the paramecia, from the platypus, and, most of all, from the humans.

She wasn't.

She was a pebble.

Every spark was a life. Every fungus, every flower, and every platypus touched the world like a pebble. They were all pebbles. They were all ripples.

And she was Littlest Death, and she had believed she was apart, separate, a carrier of a million, million sparks from one place to another.

Alone and truly filled with grief and regret for the first time in her existence, she laughed out loud.

No Hound of Joy howled with her.

"Ripples touch ripples," she said. "Some build. Some cancel."

She gathered her robes and ran along the edge of the Lake of All Souls.

When she came to the place where she had watched the first human soul walk across the surface of the lake, she stopped. Part of her wished that Ereshkigal, Baast, Azrael, or even Oldest Death could be here to see what she was about to attempt.

No. Not attempt.

What she was quite sure she was about to do. It made so much sense. Finally, she would get it right.

She turned a circle and peered into the darkness all around her—the shadowing stone, the black basalt, the branching rivers of soul leading away toward their many veils.

The darkness had always been hers. It was her metaphor—her creation imposed on Underworld.

In less than a hummingbird's heartbeat, the caverns opened upward to spring sunshine. The black floors became fields of mountain wildflowers like the ones where she had once gathered the lives of lichens.

She peered into the silvery surface of the Lake of All Souls, and the viscous silvery-blue soul stuff became clear, pure liquid. Brilliant, flashes of silver-sided trout dashed here and there. Schools of fish—all kinds of fish—big fish, little fish, chubs, perch, sunfish, trout, bass, and even bully muskies and pike swam freely and joyfully in the pure water.

She laughed.

A breeze blew, and she looked up into the brilliant blue sky and wondered what it was like to fly a kite. Perhaps she would find out, but first she had something important to do.

The lake, clear and pure now, was still the Lake of All Souls. That had not changed. The way she saw it had changed. Only that had changed, and suddenly she understood the metas she had resented for so long.

They had created themselves in order to serve their souls. It pleased her to know that Ereshkigal's wings weren't a foolish affectation. They were made to soar the heavens of an Underworld Littlest had been unable to see. The angels, too. All the winged deaths.

A thousand years, she had been wrong. So silly to have seen it so darkly for so long.

She knew she wasn't seeing it truly now, but she knew that and chose to see the beauty she now felt.

One soul, Ereshkigal had said.

She peered into the waters. The ripples she had once seen on the surface, the interacting patterns she had once seen in a rug, the chaos she had once believed came from throwing a hundred stones all made sense to her now.

The ripples spread outward on the surface, and they spread downward and upward and throughward. They never ended, and they never really began.

The first breath of the universe had brought forth life, and to give meaning to that life, it had brought forth Oldest Death.

Oldest Death was a stone. Life was a stone. She was a stone. It was all the same, and she could see what she had done—all the many souls she had placed were not misplaced. They were where they were, and she was the pebble who created the ripples that interacted with them to build them, lessen them, or bring them to the shore.

All but Paul—the one who had been meant to serve, who had one more life to live, and who had moved on.

Even that one, she now knew, had served. It had come to the moment when it knew her, saw her, went with her, and then left the cycle of life forever.

So, she would serve.

She dropped her robes and waded into the Lake of All Souls. "I am a pebble," she whispered to herself. "I am a pebble."

Chest deep in the cool water, she dove and swam toward the center of the lake. There, deep below the surface, she knew she would find a tree. On the tree would be a branch. In a hand-like branch, she would find the chalice that would make her into a soul.

A Bell Rang

A bell rang.

The sound of the bell called her.

She swam toward it, the pure water of limitless souls surrounding her, until she surfaced near a veil. She walked, knowing that on the other side waited a giant, remodeled Victorian and the flesh of the one body that had always been meant for her.

Just as the first expanding breath of the universe created life, in the first moment of every life, there is breath. Littlest inhaled, and it was the most painful thing she had done in her thousand years of existence.

Cold air burned her lungs. Fluid and a tube in her throat made her choke. Bright lights surrounded and blinded her. Though the light was not as bright as the light of the transcendent soul, it burned her eyes. She blinked, but burning pain stabbed into her brain.

She screamed.

Mucus and a thousand, thousand single-celled lives erupted from her mouth.

She sucked in a second, desperate breath.

Again, the burning, so she expelled it as quickly as she could—pushing it outward in another scream. She clawed and kicked until the tube tore free from her throat and mouth.

The effort exhausted her, so she panted.

A woman's voice called out. "Muriel! Muriel!"

Littlest didn't know any deaths named Muriel, but she didn't know all the deaths. There were too many to know them all even after a thousand years.

"She's crying! Oh my God, she's crying! Muriel! Come quick!"

Then, for the first time in all of time, Littlest Death felt a mother's touch on her raw, prickling skin.

"There, now. It's okay. Mummy's here. I've got you."

The woman pressed Littlest to her chest. The woman's soothing, quiet voice was Littlest's favorite rock. The woman's heartbeat was the lapping of ripples. Her flesh smelled of mountain wildflowers, and her warmth was the glow of the Lake of All Souls. Her caresses were more calming than tossing pebbles in the lake.

The woman breathed steadily. Hot, salty tears fell on Littlest's face.

A second voice joined the cooing of the first. "Miracle," it said. "She's a miracle."

Littlest realized the pain and the warmth and the wet—a lot of wet—meant she'd done it. All the babies had souls. Every single one. She'd done it.

Exhausted, she fell asleep wrapped in her mother's arms.

Celie Plays Bucket

Life in the flesh is hard, but it is harder if the spirit remembers Underworld, and Littlest Death was no exception. As the joys of mothers, food, air, sun, trees, grass, flowers, and butterflies filled her mind and heart, she forgot Ereshkigal, the Three-headed Drooler, Baast, Ammit, and Oldest Death. She forgot about her bucket and her foolish ambition to one day hold a scythe.

Her mothers named her Celie, and she grew and played and grew some more.

On her fifth birthday, or rather the fifth anniversary of her awakening—because her birth was still too painful for her mothers to celebrate—a bald man in a long orange robe came to their house.

Muriel Mom brought him into the backyard where Celie played in the sand with her bucket and shovel.

He looked familiar to Celie, but she couldn't remember where she had seen him, and she was busy playing with her bucket.

Celie didn't pay much attention to the bald man. He was old—really old. His orange robes smelled funny. The smell reminded her of the taste of the hard, black rose-pokies Bett Mom stuck in their roasts.

"I'm sorry you came so far," Muriel Mom said.

Celie put another shovel full of sand in her bucket. She lifted it up, but it didn't feel right, and it didn't have any sparks in it. She dumped some of the sand back out.

The old bald man said, "How far is far to see so bright a soul?"

Bett Mom came out of the house carrying a tray with grownup tea stuff on it. Celie didn't like tea, but she liked to play tea with her little tea things—especially when Bett Mom and Muriel Mom argued about who was most important for making their home.

Someday, she thought she should tell them that they both were, but just then she thought she needed some bugs to put in her bucket.

The bald man walked over to her sandbox and stood too close. He got in the way of her checking between the plastic wall of the sandbox and the grass. That's where the roly poly bugs lived, and they always played bucket with her if she wanted them to. She didn't even mind that they didn't freeze when she tapped her bucket. Rolies weren't very smart.

She always put them back where she found them. She didn't want the little lights inside them to leave.

"Well, Littlest One." The bald man got down on his knees.

Muriel Mom said, “Celie. We named her Celie.”

“A good name. An earth goddess.” The bald man nodded his approval. “Celie, I have brought you a present from very, very far away.”

Celie could see his light. It was very bright. She also saw the smaller light hidden inside his robe. She said, “The roly bugs live by your knee.”

He looked down. “I see that they do.”

“Will you please move back just a little bit?”

Muriel Mom stepped up and said, “Honey, this man is a monk.”

She said, “He smells like a roast pokey rose.”

“I’m sorry,” Muriel Mom said. “Cloves. She means cloves.”

Monk Man nodded.

“Don’t apologize,” Bett Mom said. “We agreed to raise her to know what she wants and to say what she thinks.”

Monk Man ignored her mommies. “Do the roly bugs like to play with you?”

She tapped the rim of her bucket, but her mommies, the Monk Man, and the roly poly bugs all ignored her.

He said, “That’s a nice bucket.”

Celie decided she liked the Monk Man. She smiled. “We play bucket.”

Monk Man smiled, too.

She liked the way his smile came from deep down in the light inside him. She asked, "Do you like to play bucket?"

He nodded. "So does the present I brought you."

"You have a good light," she said.

"Thank you," he said. "So do you."

Bett Mom crossed her arms and said, "We agreed not to encourage her nonsense."

Muriel Mom said, "*You* agreed. I said she's a miracle."

The Monk said, "Your moms have good lights, too."

"Uh-huh. What did you bring me?"

Monk Man pulled back an edge of his robe with one hand and reached inside with the other. When his hand reappeared, it held a wriggling, black puppy. Except for its huge paws, the whole little dog fit in his sand-brown hand.

"She's a little young for that responsibility," Bett Mom said. "You should have asked us first."

Suddenly, Celie recognized the light inside the puppy. She knew it. She didn't know from where, but she did. Celie leapt up and out of the sandbox. "Triké!" she screamed. "Triké!"

"What?" Muriel Mom asked.

"Is that his name?" Monk Man asked.

Celie reached for the puppy. "Uh-huh. Triké."

"We can't keep it," Bett Mom said.

The puppy barked, and the bark sounded like three puppies all barking at the same time.

Monk Man gently placed Triké into Celie's hands.

She hugged the puppy with all her might. Even though she'd never seen him before, she knew his red eyes were just right and his bark was perfect and he would grow up and be as big as she was. Celie started to cry, and the puppy snuggled its head up under her chin and whined its three-toned whine.

Muriel Mom said, "Something is wrong with its vocal cords."

Bett Mom uncrossed her arms. Her eyes glistened a little bit, and she half turned away. "I suppose," she said, "we could keep it."

Muriel Mom and the Monk Man laughed.

Triké yipped then covered Celie's face with slobber.

Celie's Life

Triké grew to the size of a small pony, but he never outgrew his three-part bark, and no vet would agree to try to fix his vocal chords.

Celie grew, but she never outgrew her love for the monstrous, red-eyed dog or her moms.

Time passed, and eventually so did Triké.

But he came back. At least, his light did. Over and over and over.

In all her life, Celie never stood alone. Triké always stood with her. He saved her from men who wanted to burn her clinic in Somalia. He intimidated the village elders who wanted to send her home from the slums in India. He lay beside her while she was sick and near to death in a garbage dump hovel in Brazil. Even when she spoke of love and kindness to the foolish men in suits who thought they ran the world, he walked with her—waist high and black as the Marianas Deeps—except of course for his bright, red eyes.

A lifetime passed, and Celie lay in her bed watching the quiet summer shadows cross her bedroom wall.

Someone had mowed her lawn. She couldn't see the fresh-cut grass, but the smell was heavenly.

Her body had given life to three children. She had walked five continents helping where she could. Men and women she had touched sent flowers and notes and emails from all over the world, and Lil' Muriel sat in the rocking chair by her grandmother's bed and read each and every one to Celie and her giant dog.

Lil' Muriel had gone to make some lunch. For a little bit, Celie and Triké were alone with the sunlight and the songs of the birds outside the window.

Then, Triké lifted his aging, lazy head and chuffed his three-note greeting.

A black-robed creature as ancient as the breath of the universe stood in the light beside her bed.

A goddess with wings and clawed feet stood beside him.

Both were surrounded by a brilliant, silver-blue glow.

Littlest whispered, "Oldest."

He nodded.

"Ereshkigal."

"Hello, Littlest," they said in unison.

"We all take the flesh," Littlest stated.

Ereshkigal nodded. "Every single one, when each is ready."

Littlest chuckled. "Life to understand the value of death."

Oldest Death said, “Do you want to come back to work, or would you like to—”

Littlest interrupted. “They need us. They are in a bad way. They need us more than ever.”

Oldest Death reached out his hand, and Littlest Death reached up to take it.

Triké jumped up to follow, leaving his body behind and gleefully shaking all three heads for the first time in a lifetime.

Newest Death

It felt good to leave the pain of flesh behind, to walk to a veil, to step through into Underworld. It was glorious to walk through the fragrant mountain flower meadows and along the clear, spirit streams of Underworld.

Together, Ereshkigal, Oldest Death, Triké, who once more had his normal three heads, and Littlest Death went to the Arena of Duties. There, she was surprised to find that all the deaths, meta and blank, had assembled.

Thankful to be back, to have done what each death in the Arena of Duties had done before her, Littlest Death turned to head off to her place in the tiers of seats.

Ereshkigal caught her hand and pulled her forward toward the Dais.

Left, Center, and Right held high and proud, Triké padded along behind.

Oldest Death mounted the dais. His scythe appeared in his hand. He held it high, and the infinitely sharp edge caught sunlight.

Silence descended.

Oldest Death said, "We have waited a thousand years and a lifetime for this." He dipped the scythe toward her. "Littlest Death has returned!"

Someone clapped once. Then again.

He called out to the assembled, "A new death for a new age!"

Littlest Death looked around to see who was clapping. She found the grinning face of Natchiketa. Another death began to clap—Baast. And another—Ammit. Neither could smile well, but their eyes sparkled with warmth.

Another death began to clap, and another, and soon the sound of bony hands, fleshy palms, paws, claws, wings, and scales thundered in the arena.

Confused, Littlest looked up at Oldest Death.

For the first time she could remember, and out of the flesh she could remember every time, the gaze of his full attention settled on her and filled her with warmth and joy instead of icy shame, guilt, and dread.

He waved the scythe, and the arena fell silent. "Newest death returned from life," he said, "what is your hope?"

Understanding dawned on her.

Ereshkigal squeezed her hand and let it go.

"They need us," Littlest Death said. The warmth grew inside her, and from all the spirits in the lake, from all the glowing streams, from all the rivulets and tiny trickles that lead souls back to flesh, she embraced the love and the need.

Her wings unfolded, bright and wide and encircling. Her heart swelled with the lights of all the roly polies, krill, paramecia, platypuses, flowers, trees, fungi, men, and women. Her four arms stretched out, and each hand held a tool—her bucket, her branch, her bell, and her pebble.

In an instant, all the souls of all the worlds molded her. Every ripple touched her, and she touched every ripple. She both saw herself and saw from herself. Her head became light, and her robes shifted from black to glowing silver-blue. She became compassion. She moved within the hearts of all the deaths, and all the deaths moved within her. Her ripple grew, as did every ripple she touched.

No shadow survived that moment in the Arena of Duties, and no spirit she touched remained apart from the others.

Beside her, Triké grew, and his dark coat lightened until it glowed with the same brilliance as her robes. The red fire in his six eyes shifted to palest, summer blue, and he smiled his goofy, love you smile thrice over.

Beyond the Arena, far out in the center of the Lake of All Souls, she became the brilliant glow that appeared. Ripples moved outward from the center point—from the place that had always been her center even when she had not known it. The chalice of purest white light appeared and rose upward. Beneath it, the hand of branches of the tree of life pressed upward, revealing first a wrist, then a forearm, and finally an upper arm. From within the chalice, a stream of purest new life flowed outward into the lake. The water that is eternal love and spirit began to rise.

The youngest death, who was once Littlest Death, became the meta most needed by all of life—the brightest of the bright—The Lady of the Lake of All Souls.

About the Author

Eric Witchey has made a rollercoast living as a freelance writer and communication consultant for over a quarter century. In addition to many contracted and ghost non-fiction titles, he has at this writing sold more than 140 stories. His stories have appeared in multiple genres and on five continents. He has received awards or recognition from New Century Writers, Writers of the Future, Writer's Digest, The Eric Hoffer Prose Award Program, Short Story America, the Irish Aeon Awards, and other organizations. His How-to articles have appeared in The Writer Magazine, Writer's Digest Magazine, and other print and online magazines. He lives in the Pacific Northwest because he loves the outdoors and hates to be far from a perfect trout stream.

ericwitchey.com

The Original

DUNGEON SOLITAIRE

Tomb of Four Kings

Still Available for Free
at

matthewlowes.com/games

Complete Rules
are Print-Ready and Playable
with any Standard Deck
of Playing Cards

Complete Rulebook

&

Labyrinth of Souls Tarot Deck

Available at

matthewlowes.com/games

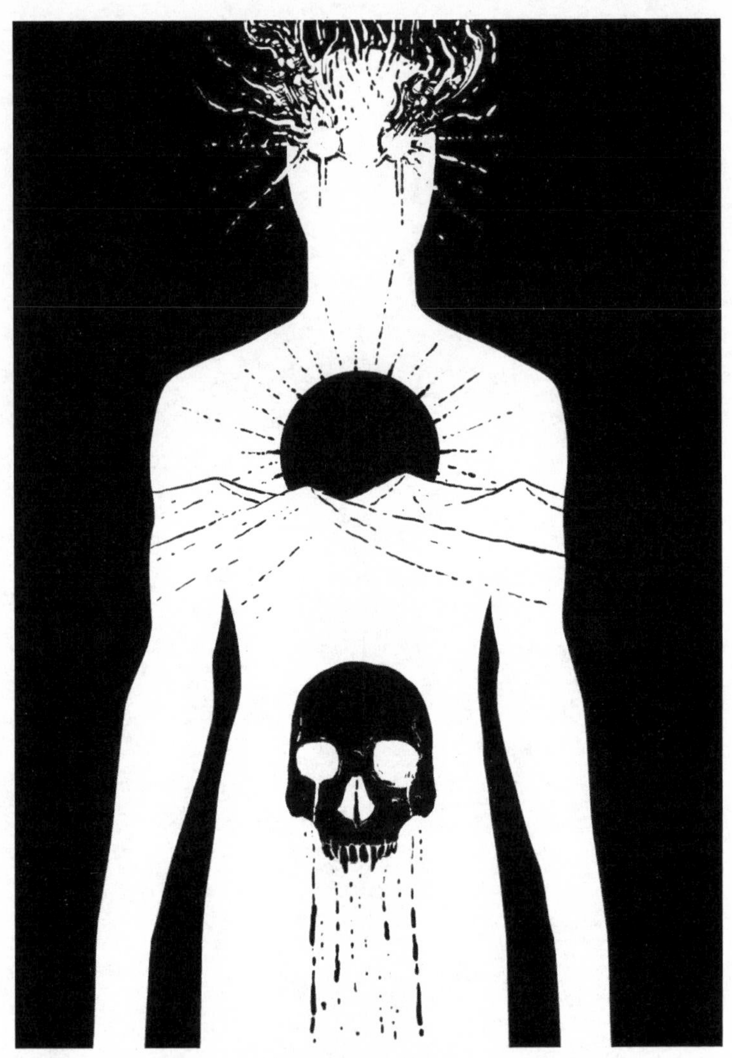